Tales of the Elastic Limit

Twelve Epic Fables

by

Howard Loring

For

William F. 'Buffalo Bill' Cody
an American original

and

John Lindenberger
my fellow traveler
who loved him so

CONTENTS

The Epic Fables

Part One PERCEPTION

Part Two INNOVATION

Part Three HISTORY

Notes and Acknowledgments

Part One
<u>PERCEPTION</u>

1
Looking Forward while Moving Backward
Or
Understanding the Primus Principle

They sat on the old, weather-beaten couch, still gazing from the back porch into the deep yard beyond. The two were holding hands and, uncharacteristically, they'd been up all night. Standing boldly in the distance, the faint silhouette of the massive magnolia tree was barely discernible in the pre-dawn gloom.

"Is it really over?" mused the husband, who knew that it was.

His wife laughed at this, understanding.

"It's a strange feeling, after all we've been through," she agreed.

He turned to look at her, still the prettiest thing he'd ever seen. Even given the years the two had shared together, he couldn't believe his astonishing luck in having had her in his life. And better yet, he knew she held the same opinion about him.

"Now that's it's done," he added, "we're the only ones who'll ever know. When we're gone, there'll be no one left aware of the truth. It ends with us."

He understood, of course, that she realized this. It had been the mission's intended outcome all along. And, given their labor was at last successfully completed, they both now knew that nothing would ever be the same again, for anybody.

"I'm most pleased," she told him. "It was an extensive undertaking to be sure, but the restored Timeline easily makes it all worthwhile. That's the important thing."

"It wouldn't have mattered either way," he pointed out. "The world would have kept spinning. No one twirling on it would have ever known the difference."

"We know, though," she noted, "and that's enough. We did a very good thing, the setting of time itself aright. I wouldn't have had it any other way."

"Do you mean that?" he asked. "We've given up much. We could have had more children, or lived a normal life without regard to any ephemeral, higher purpose."

Following his comment, the woman laughed again.

"Then we would have spent our lives wondering," she told him. "No, it's better like this. And because we've corrected the flow, it's been better for a long time now."

After that assessment, he let go of her hand. Instead, he put his arm around her and pulled her closer. She hugged him tightly, happy still in his always strong embrace.

"We actually did it," he whispered into her ear. "I can hardly believe it. It's over at last."

"Only because of you," she reminded him. "You formulated the plan and pushed it through. The Primus Principle was your idea, and you alone made that connection."

"Maybe," he reasoned, now speaking in his normal volume, "but it still took the two of us. And we were lucky, very much so. It was always far from a foregone conclusion."

By now the new dawn was breaking in earnest, and they watched in silence as again the rising sun revealed the formally hidden world, an appropriate allegory not lost on either of them.

"We should go to bed," she said, "the others will be up soon."

"I know," he muttered, still into her ear, but he held her tighter, regardless. "Just a minute more, I'm loving this. I couldn't sleep anyway, I'm too energized."

"Who says," she asked, "you have to sleep?"

"I'm loving that," he said, disentangling himself. He stood, pulling her to her feet. He was much taller but no matter, for each had always thought the other a perfect fit.

His arm around her shoulders, they walked slowly across the porch but she stopped him before they reached the house proper, turning then looking up into his face.

"I wouldn't change anything, you know," she noted, but then she laughed again, after seeing him raise an eyebrow at the heavy irony held in her simple statement.

After all, these former time travelers had indeed succeeded and, with their mission now complete, the two had already, literally and perpetually altered everything.

2
Punching the Clock
Or
How to Change Totality

The bell was near to sounding and the library's lobby was crowded with students. All were rushing, intent on reaching their next class on time. Most wouldn't make it.

She saw him first, not a difficult thing, for he was easily a head taller than anyone else there. Then, while both of them were slowly edging through the throng, their eyes met. The redheaded woman understood at once that something was wrong.

"What is it?" she asked, when they finally connected.

Looking stern, he led her to a nearby bench, where they sat. It was evident that he didn't know where to begin. She reached over and took his hands in hers.

"What is it?" she said again, but softer this time.

"We may have to postpone the wedding," he answered, as if it pained him to admit the possibility.

This statement shocked her. Not the postponement itself, but rather why such an occurrence would grieve him so. The ceremony was perfunctory and the date had been randomly picked, so neither much mattered to the bigger picture.

After all, the details were unimportant. These two young and enthusiastic academics were deeply in love, and both knew they would be in each other's lives whatever the circumstance. No, obviously something else was on his mind.

"Hank," she demanded of him, this time with stern face, "tell me why you are so upset."

Seeing her stark demeanor, at last the agitated man focused and gave her a straight answer.

"I'm sorry," he said," I shouldn't be so dramatic but the Planning Committee has summoned me. And, they want to see me badly. I've a meeting scheduled in an hour."

"The Planning Committee?" she slowly repeated, not understanding. And then, she added, "Why would they do such a thing? Does it concern your thesis?"

Here he nodded, but his words were not so positive.

"It's all that I can think," he answered. "My advisor must have passed it up without telling me, and since they want a conference they have to be paying attention, there's no other explanation. I'd have never heard from them if they had no interest."

"But that's a good thing, isn't it?" she asked, still at a loss over his strange, agonized behavior.

"Well, if they go for it," he explained, "they'd want to start simulations right away, and if so, I may not have any spare time in the romance department. The overall mission has multiple facets and they'd all require extensive run-throughs. Lots of bugs would crop up, and naturally each would have to be worked out."

"Yes, I know," she gently reminded him, "for you weren't the only one with access to your top-secret dissertation." She used her fingers to indicate quotes while saying this. Then she noted, "I helped a little along the way, I think."

He hugged her, relieved that she wasn't upset.

"It wouldn't have happened without you," he stated with gratitude, whispering the obvious into her long red hair. "I'd have never gotten anywhere otherwise. Besides all of your professional help, your confidence in me never faltered, and that mattered."

"Then why are you so troubled?" she asked him again.

"It's not the wedding, Fran," he confessed, hugging her tighter. "It's the honeymoon. I haven't told you, but I had a surprise trip all planned and ready to go."

At this she laughed, not only in relief but also in joy. She now knew that nothing was really wrong beyond set events needing adjustment. And, more importantly still, she again realized that her love for this unique man was not misplaced.

"Hank," she said tenderly, as she pulled back to look him in the eyes, "you're easily the smartest person I've ever known, but you are a colossal idiot. We'll get through this. In the larger scheme of things, it won't matter at all."

"Will you come?" he asked her, blurting it out. "Will you walk with me, I mean? And, could you linger while I have the meeting?"

"Of course," she reassured him, "I wouldn't miss it. I'm done today anyway, that's why I'm here. I was just double checking some facts, and that can wait."

"Great," he said to her, "I'd feel better knowing that you were waiting for me. I'm glad I called your office. They told me on the phone that you were on your way over."

Classes having sounded, the library's lobby was now near deserted. The two stood and exited, slowly heading to the Administration Building. It wasn't far.

"So, once the simulations are completed," she asked him, "who would they pick to go?"

He shook his head and answered, "First things first, Fran. Let's see that I'm not mistaken, assuming things that aren't really there. Could be I'm wrong about this."

"Then why would they want to see you?" she wondered.

He shook his head again.

"You got me," he mumbled, "I've no idea." Then in a louder volume, he added, "The whole thing would be kept pretty hush-hush, you know. Not that the theory itself is secret, it's been published for over two years now."

"Oh, Hank," she said, "just think if it's true. Finally a scenario that couldn't be altered. Everything would change then, and no one would even know the difference."

"That's the beauty of it," he agreed, "but now that it may actually come to pass, I'm having reservations. This is no longer hypothetical, Fran. It could really happen."

"And naturally," she correctly surmised, "you're concerned by what it could mean for us?"

"Yes," he said gravely, "but for everyone else, too. Should it even be attempted? Theorizing is one thing, but really trying it is a different matter altogether."

She took his hand, an uncommon action for her in public.

"Well, it's no longer up to you," she pointed out. "The Planning Committee would have the final say, that's what they do. And, as no such endeavor has been approved in ages, let's just wait and see, and we'll deal with it then, if we must."

16

In response, he only nodded.

Ten minutes later they sat outside the Planning Committee's conference room. There was still a half an hour until the scheduled meeting. Members of the group began arriving at intervals, all entering the venue across the hall without comment.

Fran thought Hank would soon explode. He appeared calm as he sat beside her, but she knew differently and was judging how best to alleviate the tense situation. No way his composed demeanor would last another thirty minutes, not a chance.

Then, the situation changed without her having to decide.

"Frances, what on Earth are you doing here?" suddenly asked an elderly gentleman who, after strolling down the hallway had appeared unnoticed before them.

"Why, Professor Sykes," said the surprised woman. She jumped up. Hank also stood.

The men, who didn't know each other, politely nodded. Fran was the common denominator of the trio. She quickly explained the connection between them.

"Professor Sykes is my department head," she informed Hank, as the two men shook hands. "Professor, this is my fiancé. I've mentioned him many times, I believe."

Sykes raised his eyebrows at this declaration.

"This is Hank?" he asked, pumping his arm more vigorously than before. "It's nice to meet you, young man, but I'm still at a loss, I'm afraid. Why are you two here?"

"He has an appointment," Fran answered her boss.

The Professor stopped shaking the taller man's hand, although he still held a firm grip on it.

"You are Doctor Henry?" he asked him, amazed. And then to Fran, he added, "Your fiancé, the infamous Hank, is in reality Lawrence Henry?" He then had a great belly laugh.

To this, the pair smiled, but not making the connection they failed to see the humor, for they didn't get the inside joke.

"He's the one you were helping?" Sykes continued, although he already knew the answer. He laughed again. "Wonderful," he cried, "now I know he's got his facts in order."

"But Professor," inquired Fran, still puzzled by the older man's appearance, "what are you doing here?"

"Why, I'm the Committee's Chairman," he related. "You're not aware of this, of course. The membership is strictly 'need-to-know' and our deliberations are sealed."

"You?" stated the now stunned Hank. "Professor, excuse me, but I don't understand. How could you possibly be, given that you're not a trained scientist?"

The Chairman laughed for a third time.

"It's not surprising, really," he pointed out. "Physics may provide us the means to time travel, its explanation and implementation and so forth, but that's just the beginning of the story. In the final analysis, what happens as a consequence will always fall within History's purview."

"I see," replied Hank, who suddenly did. Now it seemed apparent, for every effort intended to correct the altered Timeflow instead had always changed things. Naturally, someone had to keep a record of what occurred in-between the attempts.

"The Committee represents all points of view," added the Professor. "Nothing is overlooked, no one excluded. It's the bigger picture that we're after, the sum total."

"May I ask," said Hank, "if the Committee accepts my theory?"

Sykes didn't answer. Instead, he looked to Fran. She worked for him, and the man respected her professional abilities, which were myriad and always consummate.

"Are you sure of the intended reference points?" he asked her. "There's no doubt? You're confident the connections postulated are proper for each Timeline involved?"

She didn't hesitate.

"Of course," she said.

That satisfied him. Yes, this could all work out very well, Professor Sykes now saw. He was, in fact, much relieved by this new, unexpected turn of events.

Then holding out his arm to lead the way, he said to Hank, "Shall we, Doctor? I think we may as well start the proverbial ball rolling. You'll excuse us, Frances?"

"Of course," she again replied, but this time grinning. The retreating pair were her two favorites. They crossed the hall and entered the Committee's conference room.

She sat and waited.

It was still early but the dozen or so members, both men and women, were already gathered around a large table. Each had a thick file resting before them, and a few of these were open to reveal the contents therein, many pages of which displayed detailed graphs or complicated diagrams. Hank recognized only two of the people in attendance.

One was his former advisor, the current head of the Physics Department. The other, a renowned and well-loved Maestro, directed the School of Music. Hank knew this for he and Fran often enjoyed the university's excellent symphony, and the diminutive man was an unforgettable conductor.

"I see that all of us are present," announced the Chairman, as he crossed to his designated space at the head of the long, polished tabletop. "This is Doctor Lawrence Henry, the man of the hour," he added to the gathering. "Please, take a seat, Hank."

He did so, at the other end of the expanse in the only unoccupied chair left in the room.

"This encounter comes out of the blue for you, I'd imagine," noted Sykes, who had the advantage of the Committee's agenda.

"Yes, sir," conceded Hank, while glancing to his department head. He knew this woman well, for she was his boss as well as his mentor. Now, however, she didn't meet his gaze, being instead occupied by shuffling through the file before her.

"I now declare this meeting in session," Sykes began. "And to bring Doctor Henry up to speed, I state for the record that the Committee has been interested in his theory for some time. Further, as I just related to him outside, this assemblage represents all disciplines, so naturally some comprehend the nuances better than others may."

"I'll be happy to explain things," Hank offered.

"No need of that at this point," was the reply. "We're all conversant with your theory. It's just that some of us understand it in greater detail, as I've stipulated."

The Maestro suddenly raised his hand, effectually halting the Chair's ongoing oratory.

"A point of order, Mr. Chairman," he said pleasantly. "I've a question for Doctor Henry, if I may. Something of a more personal nature, before we begin in earnest."

"Certainly," agreed Sykes.

The Maestro smiled, pleased that his request had been granted.

"Doctor," he began, "we've been informed that your theory is quite the departure from the standard model, and this fact intrigues me. While Physics is not my area of expertise I do know something of creativity and, I wonder what was your motivation for this new breakthrough? What led you to even try to formulate such a uniquely based solution?"

This thrust momentarily threw Hank. Of course, he had thought about it, and so possessed an answer to the inquiry. Still, he'd never voiced it aloud.

"I'd imagine," he said, "it's because I have no direct, personal bond with the past. That is, given it were possible, I'd have no family to lose. You see, I'm an orphan."

"Ah, just like Frances," observed the Chairman, nodding his understanding. And then, by way of explanation to the others, he added, "His fiancé is Frances Newton, my best research assistant. She also has no living relatives, is this not the case, Hank?"

"That's true, sir," was his answer, "although we'd known each other for some time before we made the connection. However, this will soon change for we plan to marry, at least that's the current plan. Of course, we'd become our own family then."

"I see," observed the musician, "and my congratulations, young man. Thank you for indulging my curiosity, and also for being so candid in your reply. Indeed, it's very interesting to me that this natural detachment was your impetus."

"Well," admitted Hank, "I believe it was at first, as I've said. It's what originally started me ruminating about a possible solution, that is. Once begun, it was then only a matter of analyzing the many failures of the past and rethinking those attempts."

"Of course," agreed the Maestro.

"Miss Newton is a wonderful historian," Hank emphasized, "and was a great help to me."

"Yes," confirmed Professor Sykes, "I can attest that she's a superb professional. And properly, we should begin this meeting by first stating the existing context for the record. After all, if the Committee so votes, a fourth Historical Age may be instigated."

"I'm sorry, sir," Hank interrupted, "but I don't follow."

The Chairman stood. He held a page from his opened file, but he didn't refer to it. Instead, he spoke extemporaneously as if he were lecturing, which of course he was.

"The record of this planet's humanity," he began, "can be grouped into three main epochs, the first of which was the authentic, unaltered Timeline before the point of the original rupture. The second covers all attempts that were made towards correction, none of which succeeded while each only complicated the situation. The third, in which we now reside, encompasses the wars that resulted in the current moratorium placed on time travel, the very circumstance that this august Committee may soon alter by virtue of today's deliberations."

"Yes, I now understand your reference," Hank then related. "But sir, technically speaking, if the theory is proved true and is indeed successful, a new Historical Age would not result. Instead, the original Timeline, all of it from the very beginning, would be fully restored to the way it was before the first breach occurred."

The Maestro leaned forward after this statement.

"You intended to say," he asked, perplexed, "from that point when the original Timeline was initially breached? There's no need to go further back than that, surely. Not before that first incident took place, I mean."

"No, that's incorrect, I'm afraid," said Abigail Grant, who was Hank's boss, the Committee's Physicist of Record. "Second Era efforts towards restoration were often directed into the distant past, which once attempted naturally affected the original flow. As a consequence, essential connections were either not made, or were made at improper points along the way."

"It was thought at the time," Hank explained, "that such attempts could correctly reset these missed linkages. Yet they never comprehended the larger technicalities involved. The idea itself was sound, but their approach was always flawed and therefore consistently doomed the outcome."

"There is no original Timeline," Sykes stated to the Maestro, "for now it's been altered on numerous occasions." He sat before continuing with, "All we have is the record of what it should be. The problem is getting there without disruptions to the flow."

"As I've said," added Hank, "the inherent parameters were not properly understood. The phenomenon itself had never been sufficiently described, therefore no solution was even possible. And, from our point of view, these misguided past missions naturally complicated the entire scenario."

"I see," said the Maestro, "the resulting wars, you mean."

No one spoke to this observation, all being familiar with that particular part of the record. The long wars had been devastating, and the terrible consequences still lingered. This was the purpose of the Planning Committee, for its mandate was civil improvement.

In theory, Hank's theory could improve everything, and permanently. The big question was would the protocol be sanctioned? The Maestro needed clarification.

"You'll forgive me, Abby," the musician therefore said to the physicist, "I thought I was on top of this. How can you possibly send someone back to the very beginning? As I understand it, doing so is precisely what's caused most of the ongoing problems that we're dealing with today."

"That's the conundrum," agreed Grant. "Going back by definition causes change, yet to undo this change you must first go back. Hank's theory solves this paradox."

"Yes," countered the Maestro. "I do understand the basic principle, it's the extent that surprises me. It appears that I was seeing only half of the picture, I'm afraid."

"Perhaps an overview for the record, Abigail," the Chairman suggested to the Physicist.

Professor Grant nodded and complied by saying, "As we're all aware, time itself exploded after the initial breech, causing massive change to the flow by blasting parts of the existing Timeline into other eras. It was originally believed this mixing could easily be corrected by missions into the past, first to prevent the rupture, and later to earlier points of the flow, in order to head off the upcoming event. These attempts all failed."

"Yes," once again stated the Maestro. "So how would you now get back without disruption?" he asked. "To the beginning, I mean, where you've said you'd have to go?"

"The problem," the Chairman stated, "is ever cause and effect, as Doctor Grant has so elegantly explained. Travel to the past, to any point, causes more change. This modification will, by definition be unpredictable, always resulting in unforeseen ripples passing through the Timeline."

"Traveling to the point of the first blast," explained Grant, "will not correct the changes currently present in the original flow, for now they are part of the earlier record. Jumping back to the distant past in order to reset these changes does not work either, for such attempts only begets more unanticipated complications, as we've noted. That's why the Third Age was instigated, to halt all time travel thus preventing further adjustments."

"Doctor Henry's protocol proposes another strategy," the Chairman noted. "It doesn't jump to the event itself, nor to the distant past as all other attempted corrections did. Instead, it worms its way there, to the very first missed connection by backtracking to that initial event from the more recent past, where only slight change will occur."

"Again, I do understand that component," added the musician, "the so-called Primus Point. I'll leave that to those more qualified to judge. Yet, I have other concerns about this theory that deal not with the process itself, but its broader implications."

"All of us have qualms about that facet of the proposal," conceded Sykes. "We'll cover that aspect after the summation. Yet our mandate is clear, hence this meeting."

Again there was a pause, for all were aware of their shared quest, unattainable until now. This decision could change everything. It was a heavy responsibility.

"The new procedure," soon continued Grant, "embeds a team into the flow during the last attempt. This would create only slight alteration and, given the unique nature of this initial jump, the next steps would cause no change at all. This Timeframe then becomes the Primus Point, their permanently fixed home base."

"You see," added Hank, "by utilizing the standard machinery, all earlier teams returned, each ultimately causing paradox throughout the flow. However, these embedded operatives would never return. Neither would they take a machine, for we'd just send them there with our system."

Grant said, "By co-opting the hardware assigned to the previous mission, equipment now in that Timeframe, the team could then travel back to each earlier, unsuccessful attempt one by one, resetting the needed connections to the flow as they went."

"And there'd be no further disruption," surmised the Maestro, "for they'd be utilizing the machinery from this past mission?"

"Yes," Hank explained, "the time portal is there, up and running, being used by the team from the Second Age. Employing this existing hardware, covertly of course, would therefore create no new changes to the upcoming flow. The needed corrections could then be made without fear of further repercussions."

"Remember that in order to succeed," lectured Grant, "any team has to go back beyond the initial disruption, they must. If not, even if the first breech and the resulting wars are finally avoided, the original Timeline would remain altered, thus inevitably skewing the future. Nothing would really change, for what then comes would still be tainted."

"Conversely," Sykes said, "the new team would surreptitiously punch their way through the stream, as we've noted. This will cause no new changes to the flow. Once at the Primus Point, using the path of the original missions, these time jumpers would then travel backward into the affected Timeline, making the necessary corrections as they went."

"Without disruption," said the Maestro, almost to himself.

"Without additional disruption," Hank corrected him. "You see, from our point of view it's affected already, yet now, no new changes would occur as no new mission is really being launched. The missing connections could then be reset, step by step, by using the paths already created by the earlier attempts."

"Thus leaving no trace?" mused the musician, louder this time.

"And no paradox," agreed the physicist.

"I see," announced the old man. "Which brings me to another point, I'm afraid. Why would they have to remain in this new Timeframe, never to return?"

"Normally, as I've noted," answered Hank, "teams use the standard machinery. When doing so, they are by definition under containment, which means they are shielded from the surrounding flow, and this has standing consequences. The operatives don't age in the embedded Timeframe."

"Yet, when they do return," added Grant, "they once again age normally, and that fact has always caused inherent paradox within the stream. This must be avoided. Hank's protocol just sends them there and, without the containment generated by the hardware, this standing complication will no longer occur."

"So they would age as usual," inquired the musician, "because now they're permanently placed in this past Timeline?"

Hank nodded and replied, "While at the Primus Point, yes. But, while using the machine to trace the earlier paths, they wouldn't age. They'd have containment then."

Now the Maestro nodded for, making his own connection, at last he understood this complicated mission component. Again he leaned back in his seat. Professor Grant continued.

"Lastly," she summed up, "the effort must consist of at least two people, for the operations to the more recent past would have numerous problems to deal with. Once they work further back into the stream things become less complicated, and only one time jumper would do for these more primitive attempts. The second team member would then remain at the Primus Point, keeping an eye on things and assisting only if the need arises."

After this, everyone else at the table nodded.

"Very well," announced the Chairman, "let's move on. Restoring the original Timeline will have ramifications. Again, for the record, if you would, Abigail?"

"If the First Age is successfully reinstated," Grant reported, "then by extension everything will change. The natural flow, without the terrible wars, will be re-established. No one can predict what will then unfold, for the future is always unknown."

"We may not be here, you mean?" asked the Maestro.

"Well," answered Hank, "all of us would be present in the reconstructed Timeline once it reaches the point where we would naturally appear. But you are correct in the broader sense. Our circumstance would be altered, that's inherent to the procedure."

"This is a grave step to undertake," declared the Chairman, "not to be accepted lightly. However the many wars, and their terrible aftermath, would at last be avoided. And, because these alterations would occur in our past, once done no one in this Age would even know the difference."

For a third time there was silence. All present were aware of the unique protocol's potential, heavy in the extreme. Still, each member of the Planning Committee was also conscious of the mandate vested only in them, to set things right once and for all.

The Maestro again leaned in, crossing his hands before him. Then he looked Hank in the face. When the old man spoke, his words were softly uttered, but directly addressed.

"You're willing to take on this quest?" he asked.

"Yes, I can start simulations immediately," Hank answered. "The computer codes have all been written. The total process was covered in my thesis, you understand."

Yet the poor Maestro didn't understand. He wasn't the only one. Neither did Hank.

"The simulations are completed," Professor Grant informed him. "I've been running them for almost two years now. I think it's doable, that's why you're here."

This news stunned Hank. He was blindsided, taken totally unawares. But then, very quickly the true meaning of the Maestro's question sunk in.

"You want me to go?" he almost sputtered. "This was only theory for me, just a puzzle to be solved. I'm certainly not trained for such an important undertaking."

"Who is?" countered Grant. "No such endeavor has been attempted in a long time, not since the Second Age ended. You know the equipment, that's the important thing."

After this declaration, the Chairman slowly leaned forward, his fingertips just touching the polished table top.

"Of course," he calmly added, his eyes now glued to Hank's, "you'd need a second team member, as we've just discussed."

The young Doctor Henry easily made this connection. A great gift, no doubting that. Out of all humanity, after the protocol was instigated he and Fran would still be together, no matter what changes occurred in the Timeline.

"There's also Chaos Theory to consider," dryly observed his mentor, as if Hank needed further inducement. "The fewer who know of this the better. Recruiting and training someone else only exposes the mission to more variation, you know this."

"Yes," agreed Hank, who did.

"Shall we say within the week?" the Chairman then asked him. "We wouldn't need to know exactly. You certainly hold full access to the Time Lab, after all."

"We'd be quite unaware in any case," added Grant, "if your mission is successful, that is."

"I understand the implications," replied Hank, "and yes, I'm willing. I also have the team's other member already in mind. Within the week should work well for us."

"How exactly would your team proceed?" then asked the Maestro, who quickly added while looking to the Chairman, "For the record's benefit, you understand."

"As I've said," answered Hank, "the mission's code is written. The time portal will be generated here and automatically close just after we've stepped through. Lastly, the computer shuts down, pre-programmed to first delete any record of the jump."

"I see," observed the now satisfied musician, "thank you."

"Any questions?" the Chair then inquired, but there were none.

"Very well," he next stated. "All that's left is the vote. In view of this unique circumstance, I think Doctor Henry should remain for the Committee's final decision."

In the hallway, Fran was still sitting and waiting. Without warning the door across the corridor abruptly opened, and Hank came through. As always, with a glance Fran correctly read him, and so she instantly knew the news was positive.

Given his great height, only a few steps were needed to close the distance between them. She jumped up and he bent over, then the two firmly embraced. He was so tall that even on tiptoes she barely came up to his chest.

"They went for it?" she asked him, as they slowly swayed back and forth in each other's arms.

"In a big way," he answered her. "And the marriage is on, we don't have to postpone it. In fact, we need to do it pretty quickly."

At this wonderful news, she hugged him even tighter and in response he straightened, thereby lifting her off the floor.

"There is a change, though," he whispered into her thick red hair. "I'll tell you everything, don't worry. What's important now is that nothing will be altered for us."

"What is it?" she asked, unwilling to wait for an explanation.

In response, he gently put her down. Then standing to his full height, Hank suddenly looked glum. Next he laughed, unable to hold this affected demeanor.

"Turns out," he said, "my big, top-secret secret plans for after the ceremony will have to be changed. That's unavoidable, I'm afraid. Still, I think you'll like the result."

To this, she quickly cocked her head and, raising an eyebrow, without words asked him for a more inclusive answer.

"Well," he therefore slyly complied, "it seems that now we're gonna have one hell of a honeymoon."

3
Audacity Employing Opportunity
Or
Piercing the Elastic Limit

The newlyweds sat in the large bay window of the living room. This was a practical as well as a prudent choice. The house was bare, empty of any furniture.

"Do you think he's lost?" the redheaded woman, pensive and concerned, asked her husband.

He laughed at the question.

"Relax," he answered her, "the man's a genius. I think he can follow some simple directions. He's just running late, that's all."

"Do you think he'll go for it?" she next wondered.

Here he held up his hand, as if to stifle this line of inquiry.

"Don't jinx it," he said, trying but failing to appear stern. Then, seeing this humor was ineffective he instead turned serious, for he did realize how much she wanted the house. And they both knew its acquisition depended solely on the now tardy old man.

"Look," he added to his new wife, "this place is perfect, no doubt about it, but it's not essential to our larger agenda. The plan is fixed, and it moves forward no matter what. That's the important thing, the bigger picture."

She jumped up at these words and paced a few steps into the room, her back to him. He wasn't sure if she was angry. Yet when she turned, he saw that she was not.

"Sorry," she said, grinning, "but I didn't go to spy school. Still, I do know this thing may take some time and I'd like us to spend it here if we could, to build a life while we wait." She then added, while advancing slowly towards him, "It's perfect for raising kids."

He was so tall that even sitting he nearly stared her in the eye. They embraced. Then he felt her draw in a sharp breath.

"He's coming," she announced over his shoulder, after noticing through the window's mullions the car's creeping approach down the ambling, unpaved driveway.

Her husband stood at once, for she pulled him up.

"Go meet him," she quickly urged her partner, "I've got cups and a thermos of hot tea waiting in the kitchen. Show him the back deck. He'll love it."

"Not as much as you," he countered her, speaking the truth.

Soon the deed was accomplished.

"Wonderful," pronounced the old man, as the three took in the screened porch. He walked around some, gauging the view from all angles. "Yes, this will do," he added.

"It's what did it for me," confessed the redhead. "I love the entire house, of course, it's ideal, but this space is its best asset. Lots of possibilities here."

"We'll trim all the scrub," her husband dutifully chimed in, "and if we go as far as that next rise, we'll have a huge back yard."

"Most excellent for children, then," slyly observed the old man, after which they all laughed.

She led them to a built-in bench on the back wall. The cups and thermos were already there. Also a bag of cookies, for she knew how the old man savored his sweets.

"Well, congratulations," he said, while taking his seat, "for the position is yours, of course. There was never any doubt. And this job will clench the deal, correct?"

"Oh, yes," cried the relieved woman, now beaming at the news. She sat next to the old man, offering the opened bag of treats. "Thank you so much," she added.

"What did I tell you?" said her husband, who sat on the other side of the old man. The young couple was most pleased. This was precisely what each of them wanted.

Yet, it wasn't everything that the young pair secretly wished would occur on this particular day.

"However, there is a possible complication," added her new boss. "It wouldn't come into play immediately, but I still need to talk it over with the both of you. We all must to be on the same page, so to speak, with no confusion between us."

The newlyweds, leaning forward, looked to each other.

"I plan, you see," he began to explain, "to leave the university within a year or two. I shall then take a position in industry and naturally I'd want you to come with me. The money will be much better, of course, but that's not my reason."

"I don't understand, sir," the woman said. "You've always shunned the business side of things. What's changed your mind?"

The old man stood. He slowly stepped to the screened edge of the porch. He was holding a cup of tea in one hand, and his uneaten cookie in the other.

"You've heard of the Primus Corporation?" he asked.

"Who hasn't?" replied the younger man. "Everyone knows it's the world's largest company. You intend to work for them?"

"I do," he stated. "I have good reason, as I think you'll agree. But initially, before I go into further detail, I'm afraid we must first cross another bridge altogether."

He then turned, after first placing his cup of tea and still intact cookie on the ledge before him.

"I've taught each of you," he observed. "You therefore both know me pretty well. I'd hope by this time you would appreciate my veracity and sound judgment."

"Of course," she answered over her husband, who at the same instance replied, "Certainly sir, that goes without saying."

The old man then held up his hands to stifle further pronouncements along this line. He knew the two should know what they were getting into. He proposed to inform them.

"Thank you," he therefore said. "I'm pleased that you think so, for I now find myself in great need of certain help from the pair of you. In fact," he added, "I must have it to insure a successful outcome to the little scheme I've planned for the future."

"You want to hire us both?" the seated man asked him. "I thought there was only one opening in your department. And I don't think I'd make much of a secretary."

This discourse caused the old man to chuckle.

"No, you don't understand," he said. "I require assistance of another kind, something of a more delicate nature. And, it would have to be strictly off the record."

Now the young couple only smiled, still awaiting his precise meaning but nevertheless, currently acquiescing to the general thrust of his strange request.

"To begin," he continued, "I must first tell you my story. I'm compelled to, but I know it will sound fantastic, quite beyond belief. You'll think me utterly mad, I fear."

"Never," the redhead cried, jumping up. Her husband, reaching over, placed his hand on her arm. Then he pulled her closer and again she sat, but nearer to him this time.

"All I ask," the old man requested, "is that you hear me out. I've no need to demonstrate my position. You will convince each other, by virtue of your specialties."

Neither spoke to this, instead awaiting more information.

"By mere chance," he complied, "several years ago the gigantic Primus Corporation discovered something that's been kept confidential ever since. Their experts as yet don't completely comprehend its great significance, but I do. Most cognizant of my capability, they will contact me and I shall, for the sake of form, reluctantly agree to help them."

At this news, the wife looked to her husband. True to the old man's words, her face now held a look of concern but her spouse, instead wishing clarification, withheld such a hasty judgment. Therefore, his next words were direct and to the point.

"How do you know this?" he calmly asked.

The old man took a deep breath before he answered, replying softly but in a firm voice, "I'm not quite who you think me to be. I am from another age, currently trapped within this Timeframe. I'm human enough, but at present displaced here without the benefit of the advanced technology needed to solve my dilemma."

Again the newlyweds looked to each other. The old man's earlier prediction had been proved all too true. This bizarre declaration was indeed astounding.

"How?" the woman inquired, searching for plausibility.

"In theory it's a possibility, is this not the case?" the old man next abruptly asked her spouse, who held a PhD in Physics.

"I suppose," he admitted, "but the machinery involved would prove highly problematic."

"Well," the other man postulated, "then it becomes simply a matter of time and effort, yes?"

The physicist nodded at this observation, but said nothing.

The old man then asked of her, "Many innovations of the past at first seemed magical to those who failed to grasp the higher principles involved, is this not so?"

She, trained as an historian, had to acknowledge it was true.

"Time travel is a fact," the old man then flatly stated, "and later I'll give you a detailed explanation of how it's accomplished. For now, as a prerequisite, I must know if you're willing to help me in this quest. If not, then no more will be said of it, and you can always stay on at the university once I choose to leave its employ."

"That's a safe enough bet," the husband pointed out to his redheaded wife. "If they, the corporation, doesn't call, then there'll be no change for you job wise. But if it does happen as he says it will, well, that only confirms his story."

"Precisely," agreed the old man.

Now there was a pause as the pair ruminated, but it didn't last.

"What exactly did they discover?" the husband was then compelled to ask the old man standing before him.

"A time machine, of course," he answered, "or rather, the plans for one. It still needs to be built. I propose, while conveniently stalling them, to secretly construct it."

"You have your own agenda, then?" probed the tall man.

"Most assuredly," was the answer.

"And you need to do this," she tentatively inquired, as if not really wanting the answer, "because you're now trapped in this Timeframe? Why, what happened to your own time machine? Now, I'm no scientist, but I presume you had to have such a contraption to get here in the first place."

"Yes," he acknowledged, "but unfortunately I found myself in rather a sticky situation. Again, this is something I'll explain to you later. Suffice it to say that I was forced to improvise, so I abandoned my machine in order to prevent detection."

"Thus exiling you here?" asked the husband.

"For now, yes," he concurred. "Yet I first researched my options well. I knew they'd both find the plans and also have the vast sums needed to implement them."

"To build the machine, you mean?" the woman asked him.

"And the accompanying systems required," he answered, "as they are considerable. This will take a good deal of time, you understand. I'm talking long term here."

Once more the newlyweds looked to each other. They had their own secret plans awaiting implementation, and they needed this old man to carry them forward. Still, given what was at stake, the young couple couldn't afford to appear too eager.

"Why us?" therefore asked the redhead's husband, and she, not waiting for his reply added, "Yes, if what you say is true, then you could have chosen anyone."

"You are young," he explained to them, "very capable and just starting out on your own unique, now intertwined journey together. As such, each of you want nothing more than to construct a new reality for yourselves in the future, to bring about change in a positive way. And I assure you, given you're both worthy of my trust, I could choose no better."

This statement seemed to satisfy the pair.

"So, what exactly do you want from us?" asked the redhead.

"Currently, nothing at all," he explained. "You will go on with your lives, living here in this wonderful house as you've planned. However, at some point in the future I will have need of your assistance, and I wish to know now that I can count on it."

Again there was a pause. This was heady stuff, the old man knew. Yet, unknown to him, the young newlyweds already grasped the larger significance involved.

Still, timing was indeed everything, and the final facet of the situation had yet to be considered.

"This proposed agenda you mentioned to us," asked the husband, "is for the greater good?"

The old man nodded.

"It is my mandate," he answered, "a self-imposed quest that I will fulfill, in one way or another."

"And you'll explain everything," the wife asked, "in due time?"

"Gladly," the old one pronounced.

The tall man then stood. He held out his hand and, grasping it firmly she also rose to her feet. No words were exchanged but the look between them spoke volumes.

"Sir," he then said, "we didn't go to spy school but, if you want our help, it's certainly yours."

The old man smiled. He was pleased. He wasn't the only one.

"In that case," their new mentor stated, "I'll take my leave, and we'll discuss all these things in greater detail later. For now, congratulations on the house, a most excellent circumstance. I know you'll both be happy here."

"Thank you," the redhead answered him. "We hope so, too. Let me walk you to your car."

Before he exited, now with the bag of uneaten cookies in tow, the old man once more turned to view the tableau resting peacefully beyond the porch.

"You know," he casually observed, "if you trim around that centered magnolia it would then grow completely unhindered. Soon it would dominate the whole back yard, becoming a most striking specimen. Something else to think about, perhaps?"

The young couple agreed.

Later, after they were again alone on the screened deck, the newlyweds stood gazing out as the old man had done. The events of the day had played out flawlessly, as hoped. Now, unknown to him, their own time traveling mission could begin in earnest.

"He's right," the husband noted, "we should keep the tree."

"You were correct, as well," his wife added, "you always are."

He grinned at this, but it was true enough, at least this time.

"Yes, it's a win, win," the tall man mused, now most satisfied, "and all without spy school, too."

"No," she corrected, "it's a win, win, win."

He look at her, puzzled, awaiting an explanation.

"He gets us as assistants," she informed him. "I get this glorious house, as I wished. And you," she added with a smile, "will get to play with his new time machine."

Then they both laughed for, at long last, it was indeed so.

4
Moving Beyond the Elastic Limit
Or
Building by Severing Connections

"Are you sure?" the redheaded woman asked him, concern uncharacteristically held in her voice.

"Yes," calmly answered her companion, "we're more than ready, don't worry about that."

The two sat before the complicated controls inside the time machine's containment room, a heavily sealed cubicle. The scene of the impending mission was projected on a view screen in front of them. Taking up the entire wall, the image it held was huge, and also from several thousand years in the planet's past.

The man did understand her anxiety, for this was the first real operation the two of them had attempted. Yet, he identified her trepidation as unjustified. Having run through the procedure many times over, each of them knew exactly what they had to do.

"No need to stress over it," he advised her, "for the pace has gone flawlessly so far."

The redhead thought this over. He was as new at this as she was, but always cool as the proverbial cucumber. She'd hate the man if she didn't love him so much.

"I guess you're right," she offered, but not too convincingly.

He reached over and took her hands in his. She was his wife as well as his time traveling partner, hence, while being vital, this mission wasn't the only consideration. The whole situation was personal as well as professional, and that connection mattered.

"If there's a glitch, just pull me out as we've planned," he said. "The attempt may fail, but our lives will move forward. We'll just go home to live them, and that'll be the end of it."

"Yes, I know that much," she reminded him. "It's only that this particular phase is so significant, given it involves the original breech in the Timeline. Everything to come rides directly on its back, and I want to be sure, that's all."

"We can never be sure," he countered, aware that she knew this. "That's always going to be the case, every step of the way. It's all or nothing now, until it's finally over."

She nodded, for he was right, and he usually was. No wonder she loved him. Still, because she did, this endeavor was far from being just an everyday task.

"You don't even look like him," she observed. "How can you be so unconcerned? You've said anything's always possible, and the outcome is never sure until after the fact."

"It's just subterfuge and misdirection," he laughed, because it was. "I'm tall like he is and the guard, who's anxious to leave, has never even seen the guy. It'll take two minutes."

She gazed at the view screen looming before them. Several uniformed men, most milling about, were displayed in a unpretentious corridor. Only one was not idle.

"Look how young he is," she remarked, shaking her head in disbelief. "And the single person there working, too. I guess it's true that some things never really change."

This observation caused her husband to laugh louder. It was so. The soldier in the corridor, an officer, was bent over the explosive device, busy with last minute adjustments.

"Time's a ticking," her partner said, knowing this from the earlier run-throughs. "Only a minute more. Or," he added, "we can just reset and try it later, that's OK, too."

"No," she answered him, at last conceding the point. "You're right, of course. We should go."

Now there was a firmness in the redhead's voice, a determination not there before. He knew that she'd be fine and, as if in confirmation, his wife gently squeezed his hands. Then quickly releasing them, she abruptly turned back to her station at the machine's control console.

"Let's do it," she declared, adding, "No time like the present."

He stood and moved to the portal, currently deactivated. His eyes, as hers, were glued to the view screen. All but one of the men were now leaving the hallway, exiting via a door at the end of the corridor that led to the station's main staircase.

"Five seconds," she called out, while throwing a switch. The darkened opening before him suddenly came to life by quietly humming. He slowly drew a deep breath.

"Now," she said, and he, without hesitation, walked through.

Almost immediately she saw him appear on the screen, rounding the far corner of the passageway. His head was bent, and he carried a clipboard as if scrutinizing. The lone sentry, now standing guard beside the bomb, turned at his approach.

"Who goes there?" he asked, sounding most official.

"Oh," said the newcomer, "I didn't see you. I'm Spencer Hall, the station's Chief Engineer," he lied, "and I'm conducting routine spot-checks. Where's your Lieutenant?"

"He just left, sir," was the answer, "to confirm our other placements. You missed him by less than a minute. He didn't say anything about additional inspections, either."

The time traveler was unfazed, currently engaged in flipping through the clipboard's many pages.

"Well," he said offhandedly, "I told all the crew commanders this morning it was a possibility. At the operational briefing," he added. Of course, this was totally untrue.

The guard, an inexperienced soldier, was unsure of his options.

"You can call him and check," next offered the imposter, pointing to the younger man's radio.

Inside the containment unit, the redhead was holding her breath. Everything hinged on this. The rest of the mission would be easy enough but this aspect was the key itself, the Primus Point.

"No, that's OK, go ahead," the guard finally said. "My Lieutenant described you well enough, 'tall and thin, and no nonsense.' It's fine, sir, just do what you've got to do."

After witnessing this declaration, the redhead relaxed.

The tall man then stepped to the bomb, which placed before a door labeled LIBRARY. The device was in a rectangular housing. It looked like a small refrigerator.

"Here, hold this," he said, handing the young soldier his clipboard. Then he popped the digital faceplate from the front of the box. All manner of wires were exposed.

"In fact," he added, "you can mark it off for me, if you will."

"Sure, no problem," the other replied, as he retrieved a pen from behind the board's clip.

"Link to display obviously intact," the inspector reported.

"Check," said the guard, inking the appropriate box.

The bogus engineer, using his long fingers, then began to trace the bomb's mass of color-coded wiring.

"Display to timer, also," he decreed, and the guard again responded by answering, "Check."

The time traveler now had both hands inside the housing, moving the tangled wires to see the hidden connections.

"Timer to battery looks good," came next, and the guard nodded, again employing the pen while mumbling, "Check."

The spy was soon digging deeper into the mechanism's innards. He bent his substantial frame to peer inside. He was calmly working away, as if he did this every day.

"Battery to detonator OK," he said, and once more the confirmation was made.

Now the tall man went to one knee, looking head on into the device. He was currently fishing about in earnest, pushing things this way and that. At last, he drew a tool from his back pocket and thrust it in also, the better, it seemed, to probe.

"Detonator to charge is also good," he finally said, after looking up to the man with the clipboard, who dutifully made the mark, declaring for the last time, "Check."

While the guard was thus distracted, the kneeling man quickly cut this crucial connection with his wire snips. The bomb in the hallway was now deactivated. The library's contents, including plans for the time machine, were saved from destruction.

The successful saboteur then stood and, after returning the snips into his pocket, he began to reverse his process by carefully maneuvering everything back into place.

"You arrived with the original contingent, didn't you, sir?" asked the dutiful sentry.

"Yes," was the untrue answer. "I've never seen you around before. You arrived later?"

"Not too long ago," agreed the younger man. "Who'd of thought it would end this way? Evacuating the station after blowing the whole place up, I mean."

"Well," philosophized the interloper, as he snapped the faceplate back into the newly deceased bomb, "you never know what the future will bring."

This line cracked up his redheaded cohort, who was still looking at the scene on the view screen.

Her husband retrieved his clipboard from the guard, saying, "Thanks." Next the time traveler glanced to his watch. "Not much longer before we blow the charges," he noted.

"Yes, sir," the sentry agreed. He touched the radio attached to his belt. "The Lieutenant will call me just as soon as he gets the word, don't worry about that."

"Good," replied the tall man, who was already heading down the hall. He soon turned the corner and seconds later he stepped through the portal, safe and sound once more inside containment. His relieved partner quickly shut down the opening.

He crossed to her, pecked her on the cheek, then sat.

"What'd I tell you?" he asked, flushed with their success.

"Don't let it swell your head," she advised, while laughing. "We've just started, and there's a long way to go. This one was easy enough, but that's going to change."

"It's the agenda," he remarked, unconcerned by the fact.

"That's not my point," she informed him, making a face. Then she instantly turned serious, adding, "You know this. What comes next gets complicated, very much so."

"My point," he advised, "is that the game plan proceeded flawlessly. If we're careful, all of the open missions will, as well. We just have to act professionally from now on, and follow the set protocol needed to correct the alterations in the Timeline."

His wife nodded, knowing it was so.

"Should we head back now, or hang around and watch?" she then asked her partner.

"Let's wait to be sure," he replied. "Our young Lieutenant has never before returned, yet that could change. The fact that I interfered might alter the prescribed flow of events but, given there were no problems, I don't think that will happen."

"He'll blame himself, of course," she pointed out, referring to the now absent, but still hard working Lieutenant.

"Yes," he agreed, "it's what motivates him. Still, it happened in our past, so it's a done deal, regardless. We can't afford any such compunction, the plans had to survive."

She knew this too, they both did. The station itself would not endure but the time machine's designs, stored inside the installation's library, would not be destroyed. In another age they would be found and, later still, the mechanism would be built.

The lone sentry soon received his evacuation orders, which came squawking over his radio. The man was most anxious to leave, and wasted no time. Yet, the young soldier was conscientious, and he turned off the hallway's lights before exiting.

"That should do it," the tall man then ruminated. "Let's start the shut-down. We'll head home and discuss the next mission after some dinner, I'm starved."

"You're so calm," she noted, amazed by the fact. "We've just done something unprecedented, you know. It's not every day that you alter the flow of time."

"That's not true," he countered. "Choices are made constantly, and every decision creates tangible consequences. Time is never stagnant, so change is always inevitable."

"Perhaps," she conceded, "but you're talking of constructing the new, what's to come. I'm talking of changing the old, what's already been. It's not the same."

"Sure it is," he offered. "It's just your perspective is different, relative to the flow. That's the paradox in a nutshell, for it's the exact process no matter the direction."

"Moving forward while looking backward?" she asked, smiling.

He nodded as his hands started to glide here and there, dancing over the controls as he instigated the machine's complicated shut-down procedure.

"It's all about the connections," he pointed out to her. "That's the biggest paradox involved. Connections are always made no matter what choices occur."

"So, I guess," she mused, "we're not just affected by this grand paradox. Now we're currently living it. That's my big connection."

"How are we living it?" he wondered, not following her thrust.

"We now exist in our own past," she informed him, "yet our future is here, all around us."

"I hope that's so," he concurred dryly, adding, "Still, it sounds very profound, regardless."

"Just as long as that Timeframe includes your dinner, you mean?" she laughed in his face.

He turned back to the controls, and again commenced flipping switches and twisting knobs.

"Well," he said in his own defense, "some things never change."

But they always do, and totally did.

Part Two
INNOVATION

5
Reversing Gravity
Or
The Dual Nature of Everything

As predicted, the current reality was highly complicated.

The conspirators stood by an old, weather beaten bench placed under an anciently gnarled apple tree growing near a lazy country lane that meandered past a large fallow field, all of which were located at the very edge of a thriving but rustic, diminutive yet sleepy provincial town snuggly surrounded by numerous lofty, jagged and rocky mountainous peaks, each boldly striding amid smaller, undulating forested foothills.

The man was thin, and taller than the redheaded woman standing beside him, who now pointed to a row of houses in the distance, just beyond the grass-filled meadow.

"The brick one," the redhead said. "Only she is there. The boy will arrive later and her hard working, self-employed husband will appear just before dinner."

The man nodded, but then asked of her, "What does he do? I've never looked into that aspect. Is he a good businessman?"

"He is, and very innovative," answered his companion, "but betting the wrong horse, I'm afraid. His company builds direct current electrical equipment, and in a few years the area will convert to the newer innovation, alternating current. His firm, while being well managed, will nevertheless go bankrupt."

"Ah, I did know that he wants the boy to be an electrical engineer," the man noted. "That's why he pushes mathematics so, but she wants him to be a musician. Yet they both love their son, and wish for him only what's best in the long run."

He turned and stepped to the bench under the old apple tree. Very poetic, he thought, as he sat under it. Then he smiled at her.

"I want something very different for this youngster," the tall man said, stating the obvious.

Now she nodded, understanding the obvious. Much was at stake. Without further words she crossed through the field, walking towards the town beyond.

Soon enough, the lady of the house was shocked to find her on the front doorstep. Visitors at this time of day were highly unusual for her neighbors were all busy preparing dinner, as she currently was. And this woman was no neighbor.

"Hello," the redhead said sweetly, "I'm Max's friend."

"Max?" said the homeowner, now bewildered as well as surprised. "Max comes on Thursdays. Today is only Tuesday."

The young woman appeared stunned, a sham preformed well.

"Oh my," she uttered, in a deftly distressed tone. "I must have gotten the two days mixed up. I'm so sorry for arriving unannounced, please forgive me."

She awkwardly smiled, then turned to leave.

"No wait," cried the woman at the door, effectively arresting the redhead's transit. "Max is a good friend to us," she noted. And, the lady of the house didn't add, he'd certainly never mentioned such a pretty female acquaintance, either.

Highly curious by nature, this determined woman was now very interested, and she wanted details.

"Please come in," she therefore said, stepping aside. After wiping her hand on her apron, she extended it and shook the visitor's. "Call me Pauline," she pleasantly added.

"Dear me," observed the other, continuing her acting, "I don't know what to say. Max wrote and told me to meet him here, and I thought today. Now I will miss him, as I'm just passing through and won't be here on Thursday."

"Poor child," said the housewife. "Let's go to the kitchen and I'll fetch you some tea. You can tell me all about it as I make dinner."

"But I cannot possibly intrude and delay you," the young woman answered, still flawlessly playing her part. "Oh, no Pauline, I shall be on my way, but thank you. Please, just inform Max of my silly confusion regarding the dates."

"Nonsense," stiffly replied Pauline, who still wished answers, "for you shall stay and dine with us and Max will be the loser, not yourself or my family. True, we all admire him and are pleased for his keen interest in our son, but he's not here today. No matter, for my boys will want to meet a friend of his, regardless."

"We grew up together in Bavaria," the newcomer soon explained, as she sipped her tea. "Our mothers were best friends, and still are. I haven't seen Max since we were children, but his mother suggested a meeting and he suggested here."

"And where are you going?" asked her hostess, who was now returned to her former culinary duties.

"My uncle, who is a physicist, lives in Zurich," she explained, "and I am his secretary. I've been visiting my mother, but now I'm returning. Travel through Wittenberg was easily arranged, for it sits just between Bavaria and Switzerland."

Of course, besides the account's quite detailed geography, this entire scenario was totally untrue.

"And what of your bags?" wondered the cook, who was currently busy dissecting a chicken.

"I left them at the station," was the answer. "My train leaves at nine thirty. So I'm thankful for the dinner invitation, but must apologize again for intruding."

Pauline, ever the gracious hostess, once more wished to set the redhead's mind at ease, yet she didn't, for she hadn't the chance.

A curly topped twelve-year-old boy then rushed into the kitchen, slamming the back porch door behind him. He carried a book bag slung over his shoulder. Stopping abruptly, his large brown eyes opened widely at the sight of the visitor.

"Ah, Bertie, at last you arrive," stated his mother. "We have an unexpected dinner guest. She's a childhood friend of Max."

Max Talmay was a university student. After meeting the family, for two years he had been dining weekly with them and this routine would continue until he graduated, three years hence. He planned to become a scientist and, after lending Bertie many books on the subject, the boy now wanted to be one, too.

"Your hair is very red," he said to the pretty stranger.

This caused the women to laugh. The precocious boy then realized he had spoken out of turn, but no matter. He often did.

"Of course, it's not really red," he added.

"It's not?" remarked his amused mother, knowing from experience that she'd enjoy this one.

"No," he instructed them, "it's everything but red, in fact. Her hair absorbs all other colors in the spectrum but not that one, for it bounces off. That's why everyone sees it as red, but it's not her hair's true color, not really."

"So," stated the visitor, still sipping her tea, "reality is dependant only on your point of view?"

Bertie thought this over but quickly nodded. He then grabbed an apple from a bowl on the table and began slowly twirling it in his hands. Next, still thinking, he smiled.

"What you should be seeing," his mother admonished, "is your instrument. You have sufficient time to practice before we eat. And don't spoil your appetite."

Soon, scratchy scales were emanating from a distant violin.

About an hour later, the man of the house finally arrived. During introductions he insisted the visitor call him by name, Hermann. Then, dinner was served.

"Bertie, how was school today?" Hermann asked his son, who answered him with, "Boring."

This observation was ignored. Bertie, he knew, was easily bored. Yet his father also knew the boy did enjoy certain subjects.

"And how's your math coming?" was the next question.

"Fine," was the droll reply, "but it's getting harder, not easier."

"Perhaps you should concentrate more on music," observed his mother, seeing an opening to press her preference. Still, her current concern did deal with mathematics. Given the unexpected company, an extra division of chicken had occurred in the dumplings, with a proportional and equal addition of dough.

"But music is also hard for me," Bertie commented, yet all too sadly. Then he laughed aloud, unable to hold his affected, stricken demeanor. Then they all laughed.

"Is your uncle really a physicist?" Bertie asked the newcomer.

"Yes," she answered, "are you interested in physics?"

"I want to be a scientist," he declared without hesitation. And then, he added, "Physics is fun, but you need to know math. I'm really not that good with numbers."

"That's nonsense," scoffed his incredulous father, "your ranking is always above excellent."

"But it's hard for me," the boy said again, seriously this time.

"Nonsense," Hermann repeated. "You simply need to apply yourself. I've told you this many times."

No one spoke for a moment and there was an awkward silence, then Hermann asked the dinner guest, "Is this not so? Does your uncle not apply himself? And does he not enjoy it, being paid for something he likes to do?"

All eyes at the table then turned to the redheaded visitor. Here we go, she thought. This was it.

She then commenced her time traveling mission in earnest.

"My uncle," she began, "is a fine scientist. That means he thinks in a special way, a way he's learned to employ for a purpose. He looks at things differently."

"But he uses math?" asked Hermann, not seeing her point.

"Yes," the woman concurred, but with a reservation. "It's true, he describes reality using equations and therefore has to be knowledgeable of them, but that's not really his aim. He deals instead with ideas, new ways of describing things and, he can always assign his students to perform the needed math for him."

Hermann raised his eyebrow at this shocking statement. His wife, not knowing his further reaction, stopped her chewing while waiting to see. The redhead was unfazed.

"Of course," she added to Bertie, "your father is quite correct, for you must become proficient to be a teacher in the first place."

"Indeed," agreed Hermann, now satisfied.

With this, the lady of the house commenced her chewing.

"You never answered my question, Bertie," the redhead reminded him. "You say you want to be a scientist. Is not physics a fine branch of science?"

"Yes, but it's been done already," Bertie said to her, "the biggest things, I mean. Isaac Newton long ago figured it out, and there's nothing new to know. Max has loaned me many books on Newton and they all say as much."

"There are new facts to learn about electricity," dryly observed Hermann, who could judge. "There's always something to discover. This will never change."

"But that's my point, Papa," argued Bertie. "All the basic ideas are formed already, with only the details left to unravel. And I want to discover big things."

"Like what?" asked his mother, "I don't know what you mean."

"Like gravity," he answered her. "Before Newton, no one knew why things fell, they just took it for granted. He changed this outlook, for his equations explained it."

"Did they?" asked the redheaded guest. "Perhaps, from one point of view, at least. But there are other points of view, you said so yourself earlier today."

This was true, but what was the connection, Bertie wondered?

"I don't understand," he therefore countered. "Thanks to Newton's endeavors, gravity's existence is now quite obvious. What other way is there to look at it?"

"Well, you must describe it differently," she explained.

Bertie looked to his father but, while looking back, the now amused Hermann said nothing.

"How?" finally asked the baffled twelve-year-old.

"Suppose your neighbor is standing on his roof," she replied. "Gravity holds him there, according to Newton. He has an equation to describe this, yes?"

"Certainly," agreed Bertie, "and he also states that an unmoving object remains at rest unless some outside force acts upon it, and there's an equation for that, too."

"Suppose he steps off the roof," she asked, "what occurs then?"

"Why, he falls," said Pauline, "even I know this."

"But how does he change?" the redhead countered her, while looking directly at the boy. "Describe what happens to him. Using the terms of physics, I mean."

"The force of gravity," explained Bertie, "pulls at his mass until its effect is negated by the ground's mass, and Newton's equations describe this condition, also."

"So he moves?" she probed.

"Why, of course," laughed Hermann, "that's a direct observation that anyone may see."

"But there's ever two ways of looking at things," she responded. "Your vaulted math demonstrates this. They're called equations because they equate."

After this declaration, Hermann raised both his eyebrows.

"Oh, dear," said the woman of the house, "you've lost me now."

The redhead smiled at her hostess. Pauline, a talented pianist, knew nothing of science. Yet she was intelligent, and the point involved really wasn't that ephemeral.

"It's simple," her guest related, "for in any equation, something always equals something else and each side is just a different way of describing the identical concept. Two plus two equals three plus one. Both are the same thing."

"Oh, I do see," answered Pauline.

Now Hermann smiled, his eyebrows no longer raised.

"Motion is the greater part of physics, is it not?" the redhead next asked the curly headed boy.

He nodded, for it was so.

"Newton's Law," she continued, "presupposes downward motion for that's exactly what gravity does, it pulls something down. Yet, is it not also possible to depict the same exact phenomena but in a totally different way, from another point of view entirely, simply by supposing instead that no downward motion occurs? How would you then define what happens to the man who steps off his roof?"

"But this is absurd," protested Hermann. "Gravity is real enough. It can be demonstrated, it's demonstrated every day."

"But she's not saying that gravity isn't real," deduced Bertie, easily understanding her thrust. "She's saying that you can describe it differently, that's all. The same example of reality, but from another perspective, that's what she means."

Here, the redhead, still smiling only nodded.

"How would you do that?" asked Pauline who, although trying her best to follow, was lost once more.

"Well," said Bertie slowly, reasoning aloud, "if the man doesn't move to the ground then the ground must move to him, there's no other way that fits the facts."

"Precisely," noted the redhead, who now was most satisfied.

"But what does that mean?" asked Hermann, currently the one confused. "How can the ground rise up? It's fixed in place, and clearly doesn't shift its given position."

"But the Earth does move, very much so," she noted. "It spins on its axis and flies through its orbit. If we're unaware of this motion, does that mean it doesn't happen?"

Now, no one spoke. All were considering. All but the redhead.

"What would it signify?" she then almost whispered to the boy. "Think of the equation. What would equal what?"

"Well," Bertie ruminated again, "on one side you'd have gravity, that's downward motion. On the other side you'd have upward motion. That's acceleration, I guess."

"Yes," she concurred, holding her breath, "and that means?"

"Gravity equals acceleration," he quickly pronounced.

"Very good," she observed, breathing once more. Then she added, "Perhaps equations aren't dull, after all. Perchance there are still big things yet to discover."

"Just as you said, Hermann," Pauline smiled at her husband.

"Yes," noted the boy, "this outlook is most interesting."

"And dinner was most delicious," added the redhead. "Thank you all, I'm very pleased that I came. In payment, I'm washing."

"You certainly will not," announced Pauline. "It's a quarter to nine, and we shall walk you to the station. The dishes will wait."

"No, please," the redhead declared. "I've already arranged for a railway porter to come here and fetch me. He should arrive soon, I didn't realize it was so late."

As if on cue, there was a knock at the front door. Bertie dutifully went to answer it. Sure enough, a very tall, thin uniformed man stood on the porch.

"Is this the Einstein household?" he inquired.

"It is," Bertie responded, "are you from the train station?"

"I am," replied the man, who wasn't really a railway employee. "Are you Hermann Einstein's son? I have many acquaintances who work for his electrical firm."

This scenario was also untrue, but Bertie didn't know that.

"Yes," the boy answered, "I'm Albert Einstein."

The tall man then smiled at him, slowly nodding as he did so.

Soon, goodbyes were exchanged on the doorstep.

"Remember, Bertie," the redhead advised him, before she took her leave, "reality can be defined in many ways. You need only think differently, and so conceive new connections unknown to others. The equations will follow."

The Einstein family then watched from the stoop as the redhead and her escort walked away, and soon they saw them disappear around a nearby corner.

"Dear me," decreed the lady of the house, slowly shaking her head, "our friend Max sure lost out with that one."

"You did very well," the man said to his partner, as the time travelers walked through the field. "I mean it. You handled yourself most professionally."

"Thanks," the woman responded, pleased that he thought so. Then she asked, "Was it really necessary? Would he not have made the proper connection on his own?"

"Perhaps," the tall man mused, "it's more than possible. After all, everything's relative. Or it will be now, at least."

"Relatively speaking, you mean?" she asked.

They both laughed at this banter but neither spoke further. There was no need. At the edge of the field, they turned and walked down the meandering lane, past the old, weather beaten bench still resting under the anciently gnarled apple tree.

Poetic indeed.

6
Clash of the Redheads
Or
Methodology and Firmly Fixed Jargon

The buckboard moved at a leisurely pace, with a slow but constant clipping of the horse's hooves reverberating off the narrow, cobble stoned street. About time, she thought, after finally noticing its creeping approach from around an adjacent corner. Naturally, she was relieved thereby, but concerned nevertheless.

The mission was just starting, and already it was off schedule.

"Why so late?" asked the redheaded woman, as she climbed aboard. "What's happened? Have the crates been delayed?"

"No," answered the tall man holding the reins, "as was reported, they arrived this afternoon. The problem was elsewhere, I fear, something I missed. The good bishop's horse threw a shoe several miles out, and he had to lead it in on foot."

The woman thought this over. Clearly, the unexpected development was not judged a setback to the mission. In any event, it wasn't her call to make.

"Well," she replied, "at least there's been time to unpack."

They both laughed at this, each seeing the irony and the double meaning. The many accounts describing this day were of bones everywhere, spilling into the hallways from the over-crowded rooms. And also, their mission dealt directly with time itself.

Washington City, the young nation's new capital, was small but growing. This engendered a ragged appearance with much construction everywhere in evidence. These seemingly haphazard endeavors now begat never-ending piles of building supplies amid giant mounds of excavated dirt, which quickly became a mucky runoff after the afternoon rainstorms so frequent this time of year.

As well, being located in a drained swamp, the place was sticky with humidity and heavily infested with mosquitoes, leading the beleaguered citizenry to appear haggard and unkempt. Yet, various official structures were slowly being completed. The never ending, ever-pressing business of state plodded on, even among the surrounding chaos.

The pair soon reached their destination, an isolated mansion atop a muddy rise that boldly stood amid the rubble that was the growing capital. Due to the lateness of the hour, sentries bearing muskets stood guard on either side of the front door, which was open in hope of encouraging a draft. There was none.

"May I help you?" asked a functionary who, having seen their approach had walked out to meet the strangers now standing on the large, columned portico.

"Good evening, sir," replied the redhead's companion. "We bear important dispatches for the President." Handing over two large envelopes, the taller visitor then added, "These sealed documents are our letters of introduction."

The papers in question were faked, of course.

The man, an official of some kind, looked to the first envelope and scrutinized its bold, handwritten provenance. Then his eyebrows shot up. Next, without examining the second letter he extended his arm, beckoning the pair inside.

"Wait here, if you please," he instructed them, once the three had entered the grand foyer. "President Jefferson may wish to speak to you. I'll know in a moment."

"We could just drop off our pouches," observed the redhead.

The attendant, now overly gracious, slightly bowed.

"That will be up to the President," he related.

So it was, and sooner than the time travelers had expected, the man himself arrived by rushing down the carpeted hallway. His red hair was pulled into a tail by a large black ribbon, but he was in shirtsleeves without frock coat or vest. He carried a now opened letter of introduction, waving it excitedly before him.

"Are you really an anatomist?" he cried, while grasping the man's hand and shaking it vigorously. "You've studied under the great Monsieur Cuvier? You carry correspondence from my esteemed acquaintance in faraway France?"

"Oh, no, Mr. President," answered the stranger. "My name is Edward Patrick, and I'm a scientist trained under your good friend, the eminent Joseph Priestley. He died of late in Pennsylvania, at his home outside of Philadelphia."

"Yes," admitted Jefferson, who was well aware of this sad occurrence, "a great loss, to be sure."

The conspirator then indicated his companion, adding, "This is Ellis Alexander, and she bears your dispatches from France."

"Indeed," replied the startled Chief Executive, now taking her hand. "Alexander sounds Scottish, madam. Are you French?"

The woman, playing her part, laughed at the question.

"It's Miss Alexander, Mr. Jefferson," she coquettishly corrected the now embarrassed President, "and I assure you that I'm very much an American. My uncle, who also lives in Philadelphia, is a naturalist trained under the late John Clayton. He was an Englishman who moved to Virginia long before the war."

"Yes," Jefferson offered, now smiling, "I know who he was."

"My uncle," she continued, "frequently corresponds with the famous zoologist, Joseph Banks, and through him with Monsieur Cuvier, as well as many other natural philosophers in Europe. These packets of personal letters and scientific papers were therefore sent to my uncle for safe transit, and I bear them now."

Here she indicated a carpetbag currently resting beside her.

"But this letter says that you are trained," observed Jefferson.

"True, I assist my uncle in his endeavors," she explained, "helping with his specimens and correspondence, and so forth. This naturally includes comparative anatomy, and I have become aware of much as a consequence. I enjoy it."

"Well," replied the now satisfied President, "I trust you'll enjoy this visit, too. And, given the hour, you must both stay for dinner. I won't take no for an answer."

He then led them down the hallway from whence he had come. While doing so, he opened the second sealed letter of introduction and quickly perused its contents. Soon though, he stopped short, halting the time travelers that followed him.

"Ah," he said, "you carry just what I've been awaiting, Edward. You bring me Doctor Priestley's last notes concerning the new state university to be built in nearby Charlottesville." He then added, "I may call you Edward, may I not?"

"I'm most honored, Mr. President," uttered the imposter, although the many documents he carried, as well as those born by his cohort, were genuine enough.

"His friends," noted the redhead, "call him Ward."

"Wonderful," stated Jefferson. "I shall also. And, as an intimate of the good Doctor Priestley, he should enjoy this evening as well, given Bishop Madison is here."

This statement caused the taller man to laugh.

"But I'm no theologian, sir," he apologized. "Joseph Priestley, as I'm sure you are aware, was a great scientist as well as a churchman. I assisted him in that vein only."

Now the President laughed.

"All the better," he answered, grinning widely now. "You'll see, the both of you will. Follow me to my office, if you please."

Soon the bones appeared. As stated in the record, they were everywhere, hundreds of them, placed on tables and desks, across chairs or simply, as there was no more available space, dispersed upon the floor. Most of them were fairly large.

"Goodness me," gasped the redheaded woman, still acting.

"What's that?" said a gentleman standing in the corner of the Chief Executive's command center, as if trapped there by the sheer number of assembled specimens. He was residing before an enormous, opened crate filled with straw, the last of several lately sent by the now famous explorer, William Clark. The interrupted man had been shifting through the crate's inventory, a thick stack of parchments held in his hands.

"Aren't they magnificent?" gushed the President, while signifying the just liberated items. Then he added, "Good news Jamie, we have unexpected dinner guests and luckily they are both trained in Science. I believe some claret is in order."

Introductions were quickly made.

James Madison, cousin to the well-known politician of the same name, was the current Episcopal Bishop of the Diocese of Virginia, the first American born cleric to hold that esteemed office. His bishopric being so close, he frequently visited the new federal city to confer on the President's current obsession, the proposed state university. Of course, as both families were neighbors, most of the Madison's were Jefferson's good friends but this churchman was his oldest and dearest companion since childhood.

"These fossils arrived today," the excited President explained, although the time travelers, being well briefed, already knew this. "The great western expedition is barely over," he next related to them, "but I've sent poor Captain Clark off again, I fear. This time, he's busy investigating Doctor Goforth's newly discovered site at the now legendary Big Bone Lick, which is located astride the broad banks of the Ohio River."

The four now stood around Jefferson's desk, which held several curved pieces of skull, two different sized tusks and various sections of large jawbones. All were a deep tan color, even the ivory. Indeed, they were impressive.

As the group sipped their claret, the bishop pointed to a tusk.

"I've seen one of these at Monticello," he said to Jefferson. "You have several there I believe, is this not so Tommy?" Then, after suddenly remembering the proper decorum, he injected, "Mr. President, I meant to say."

They all laughed at the comment, and Bishop Madison's old friend Tommy then proposed a toast.

"To Captain Clark," he proclaimed.

"Here, here," said the cleric, adding, "and to knowledge itself."

"Yes, and to Science," quickly followed the tall time traveler, whereupon all eyes then fell to the redheaded woman.

Holding forth her glass, she boldly stated, "To discovery, and the unending drive to undertake it."

"To discovery," the men agreed.

"And, it's true, Bishop Madison is correct," the President then explained to the newcomers. "I do have several examples of mammoth on display in the entryway at Monticello, but they are from the earlier expedition. These newer specimens were discovered only of late, uncovered in another part of the Lick."

"But Mr. Jefferson," the woman noted, "I'm afraid these items are not artifacts of the woolly mammoth."

This bold statement took the President aback. He'd been interested in such things since he was a boy. The new samples, he thought, were easily recognizable.

Undaunted, she indicated a section of jawbone that was over a foot in length. It held a row of large serrated teeth, each one containing distinct, raised bicuspids. Taken together, they resembled a jagged ridge of mountainous peaks.

"Mammoth teeth," she lectured, "are flatter, as the molars of a horse, only much larger. These come from another member of the elephant family, as the great Monsieur Cuvier has recently demonstrated. He has named them mastodons."

"Oh, dear," mumbled the bishop, who of course was fluent in Greek, and so was capable of translating the term.

"Nipple tooth," she said, running her finger over the ridges.

At first, Jefferson didn't respond. Soon though, in spite of himself, the corrected President laughed aloud. Next, he blushed.

Thankfully, at this point dinner was announced.

The group slowly filed into a dining room across the hall, after gingerly stepping over the numerous items placed about the floor.

As was his custom among close friends, the President then served his guests himself, employing a nearby, fully stocked table. The meal was expertly prepared and included macaroni and cheese, a dish Jefferson savored. He'd discovered it years before, when Congress had sent him to France after the Revolution.

This fact was quite apropos, given the intrinsic, diverse nature of the new nation. After all, Jefferson was the very epitome of the well-educated and wealthy upper class landed gentry, and as such he had been charged with an essential task deemed vital to the country's nascent future. Yet from the very heart of France, this elegant man had retrieved for the masses an imported Italian staple, tasty and cheaply made.

It was then that he had met Georges Cuvier, the greatest naturalist alive. A zoologist by training, Cuvier's chief fame lay in his use of Linnaean principles to classify the animal kingdom. Living a generation earlier, the towering Swedish botanist, Carl Linnaeus, had used his method mainly to catalog plants.

As an inherent prerequisite, the now ennobled Baron Cuvier had been compelled to invent comparative anatomy in order to construct his new taxonomy. Over many years, Jefferson had sent him numerous ancient specimens unearthed in North America, and these became the basis of the vast collection soon to be housed within the French Natural History Museum. Cuvier's classification system was therefore unique, for it encompassed both fossils and living animals.

"What do you make of Captain Clark's artifacts?" the so-called Ellis Alexander then asked of the bishop, feigning polite dinner conversation. "Are these magnificent beasts really extinct," she continued, "or are they currently living and just undiscovered, hidden somewhere in the far west? Are there still roaming herds of mastodons alive today, do you think?"

Madison smiled at this thrust, understanding her intent.

"What you are really asking," he retorted, "is do I consider the Earth older than biblically believed. And also, why would any animal created by the Almighty be permitted to die out?" Leaning forward, he then added, "Simply put, is the Bible infallible or mere metaphor, and is this whole idea truly nothing but blasphemy?"

Now the redheaded woman smiled.

"Yes," she replied.

"Don't answer that, Jamie," screamed the President, holding up his hand, "not yet at any rate, I need more claret first. Anyone else?" he asked, laughing while reaching for the nearby bottle. Having eaten his pasta, Jefferson was finished with dinner and in truth, he never consumed much at any given meal.

As the others were still dining, they each politely declined.

"I do believe your Science has value," the bishop continued, unfazed by the outburst, which was a common enough occurrence from his old friend. "Yet I also believe the Scriptures to be true, given the proper context is employed. And, as to why God does what He does, well, I'll just take that on faith, and leave such weighty decisions up to Him."

"Here, here," said the male imposter, who currently was only posing as the messenger Ward Patrick. "After all, the two disciplines are totally different in both character and intent. I see no conflict between them."

"Religion and Science, you mean?" inquired Jefferson.

"Yes, Mr. President," answered the time traveler. "All other standardized disciplines, including Theology, seek only the truth. Science, of course, does not."

This striking comment stunned the two Virginians. They looked to each other as if to confirm that both of them had heard the same statement. They had.

"Science does not seek the truth?" asked Jefferson, perplexed. "I thought Science stood for that very purpose, to redefine what's true. Am I in error by holding such a stance?"

"I'm afraid so," answered the redhead, "if you believe as Ward does, or Mr. Priestley, his mentor. Yet currently, the parameters of Science as an established method are still in debate. Not everyone accepts the interpretation they embrace."

"I'm quite lost," declared Madison. "How can Science not seek truth? Is this not its function, to rectify previous errors and so demonstrate the correct state of affairs?"

Ward put down his knife and fork. He then slowly wiped his mouth with his napkin. Next he placed it beside his plate, signifying his meal was also completed.

"It's simply a matter of definition, gentlemen," he stated. "Science is only a tool as are all disciplines, and every discipline such as History or the Law employs set jargon, the specialized language used therein. Yet, this fixed terminology must be first universally accepted in order to avoid utter confusion."

"Theology employs much jargon, is this not so?" asked Ellis of the bishop. "A gospel is not an epistle, nor is The Old Testament the Canon. These provisos are agreed upon by all theologians and other experts in the field, are they not?"

"Yes, that's correct," he granted, not sure where she was going.

"So it is with Science, or rather it shall be," offered Ward. "As my companion has so eloquently related, it's still being discussed but the outcome is clear, at least in my humble estimation. Science will become the only discipline not concerned with truth, and this standard will grant the method a greater power to discern reality."

"Now I'm lost," said Jefferson, again laughing as he stood. He began to circle the table, refilling his guest's claret glasses, this time without asking their preference. No doubt the President was enjoying the evening thus far.

"Science," explained the woman, "is based on fact, not truth."

"But that's preposterous," boldly argued the bishop. "The two terms are quite interchangeable, and by definition mean the same thing. Facts are certainly true."

"By your elucidation, yes," she conceded. "But such a stance denies Science, as an established discipline, the use of its own jargon. Facts are scientifically distinguished from truth, which is ephemeral and therefore always open to debate."

"How so?" inquired Madison.

"One man's truth may not be another's," she answered, "hence, by its very nature the concept cannot be universally defined."

"For instance, within the Law," suggested Ward, "the truth is very much in doubt. The prosecution declares a man guilty while the defense proclaims his innocence. Legally, it's then up to the jury to define what's true and what's not."

"Yes," cried the President, who by now had resumed his seat, "I take your meaning, sir. In such a case, the definition is indeed fluid, and would rely solely on the argument's merit. That, and the advocate's presentation, of course."

"It's the same with History or Theology," added the woman. "You cannot simply state, to use another example, that Christ was the last name of Jesus, or that King George could not read. Without the proper protocol, such a stance would have no credit, that is, it wouldn't be creditable by any rules set by the discipline."

"Yes, it would be incredible," again agreed the bishop.

"Look at it this way," Ward said. "Any clear morning at dawn you can see with your own eyes that the sun rises, always climbing, and then, past noon it will fall once more towards the horizon. This is an undisputed fact, a direct observation, yet does it mean it's true that the sun actually moves about the earth?"

"Well," stated Madison, "it's true that everyone used to think along this line, that's accurate enough."

"But now we know differently," continued the woman. "Yet, will the fact that the sun does not move negate what you saw? Does it become less of a fact?"

"No, I suppose not," the bishop conceded.

"No," she agreed, trying to make the connection, "what it means is that you don't have all the facts."

"The difference," added her confederate, "is that facts are demonstrable things while what's true is only someone's point of view. Interjecting truth into the equation simply clouds the issue, and always will. Just ask Galileo."

"He's got you there, Jamie," chuckled Jefferson.

The bishop only grunted in response but at last he made the connection, and he saw the larger point involved. The official imposition of truth may have been a fine thing in the past for it had held civilization together, but this rigid stance undeniably stifled forward progress. That fact couldn't be denied.

"So," next wondered the President, "using your interpretation, are you saying that no scientist can believe his ideas to be true?"

"They would be factual," answered the woman, "not true, per se. Any principled scientist who states 'my theory is true' is really saying that it's 'true to the facts.' Truth as an ideal must fall within the field of Philosophy, not Science."

"As I said before," related Ward, "the two disciplines are quite different in nature. Or rather, they should be. And, it's my hope that this enlightened view wins out."

"A position held by your mentor, also," stated Jefferson, referring to the late Joseph Priestley. The brilliant Englishman, a towering man of letters, literally had been shipped out of his native country for nothing more than his astounding ideas. At the time Jefferson was Washington's Secretary of State, and he had immediately instigated a long and warm correspondence with the exile, covering an eclectic agenda of subjects.

Yet, at mention of the immigrant, the prelate grunted again. Priestley, aside from his vast scientific and philosophical writings, had been quite the effective and well-known dissenting churchman. He'd virtually invented Unitarianism, and he alone had first introduced the new denomination into the country.

"Yes," agreed the tall time traveler, ignoring Madison's reaction. "Priestley greatly advanced the establishment of Science as a factual discipline. His new style of notation for chemical elements has done much for standardizing that field."

"Use of this new jargon," noted the redhead, "permitted him, enabled him even, to identify previously unknown components in the very air, such as oxygen. And, many people greatly enjoy the tasty soda water he concocted, a tangible example of something produced by this now set method. His early work in the field of electricity, also granted by virtue of the scientific process, rivals that of Mr. Franklin himself."

"His bold ideas on teaching, and education in general," added Jefferson, "are most insightful, as well. I know this first hand, for we exchanged many letters over the years in regards to Virginia's new university. He was quite astute."

The bishop grunted for a third time, but leaning forward he then sternly decreed, "I know where you're going with this, Tommy, and I won't be moved."

After the comment Jefferson's demeanor instantly changed, for he correctly read the intended meaning behind the statement. Unbeknownst to him, the time travelers also understood. The issue was the structure and purpose of the new university, and the President never made light of that subject.

The Virginians had a stiff divergence of outlook regarding the proposed state institution. Also, as both were members of the Board of Visitors, the official committee charged with the details involved, this long-standing but deeply held difference of opinion had continually derailed any finalized plans for the new entity. As a consequence, the university's future was currently in Limbo.

Jefferson wished a school without formal religious affiliation, something he distrusted as a matter of course. The bishop naturally disagreed, and he objected most strenuously to the stance of his oldest friend. The pair were at an impasse.

The President's dream was to provide his state a public university unlike those heretofore, free from theological dogma of any kind. Dedicated not to God Almighty but to knowledge itself, this novel institution would embrace such diverse arts as Architecture and Applied Engineering, or various branches of Philosophy including Political Science, plus Astronomy, Botany, the new Zoology, and of course, the Law. This innovative view was an astonishing posture given the times for, as other establishments of higher learning were primarily training grounds for the ministry, additional courses offered at these schools were only auxiliary to this chief purpose.

Jefferson, as always, sought something quite different in nature. He wanted another approach altogether, with a bold statement of intent that was currently untested. He desired for his beloved state a university totally devoid of contemplations of divinity, one that would match the courageous audacity of the new, uniquely formed nation.

Madison thought such a posture would insure nothing but a negative, second class reputation, something unworthy of Virginia. Yet he was no religious fanatic, and for all of his vibrato he did believe that personal dogma should have no sway in terms of politics. Seeing its value, he fully embraced the separation of church and state, but being a man of unbending principle, he only wished what was best in the long term, and he could not bring himself to agree with Jefferson's preference.

"We're both on the university's Planning Committee," the President then told the visitors, by way of explanation. "There are still many contingencies left to consider, I'm afraid. And, it's true we view certain inherent problems differently."

Of course, the time travelers knew the situation. They had researched the bishop's oft stated position well. It was their official mission to change his mind.

"I understand, Mr. Jefferson," next asked Miss Alexander, thereby breaking the awkward silence following the last declaration, "that you've designed numerous buildings for the projected university, is this not so?"

"Oh, yes," he responded, suddenly animated. He adjusted himself, sitting forward in his chair, saying, "I've completed plans for several, and have sketches of many more. They're in my office," he added, "would you care to view them?"

"Don't expect a proposal for any Chapel," opined Madison.

"No," countered Jefferson, "but the Library drawings are finally completed, and that, not a church, will be the focal point for students and instructors alike."

Once more the good bishop grunted, but Jefferson didn't relent.

"I have but one year left in my term, Jamie," he said. "Then it's Monticello for me, and the university will be my first and foremost concern. You must yield, and concede that another religious school is unneeded, that's the whole point."

"Such an arrangement would be unprecedented," declared Madison. "It's not acceptable by any standard. This discipline of Science may be a grand tool but it's only one of many, and you must also teach Religion and accept God's sanction."

Jefferson sighed and sat back in his chair, again resigned to the stagnant status quo. Still, knowing Madison's good intentions, he felt no malice towards his dear, old friend. After all, the brick and mortar work of the university remained years in the future, and the two of them would surely live to debate another day.

Yet the President found himself unable to let the moment pass.

"I take it, young man," he surmised, "you agree with your mentor that such a scientific approach is the best possible avenue for the advancement of education."

The time traveler only nodded, unwilling to upset the poor bishop further. However, his redheaded colleague now sensed that they were close to achieving their goal, and wished him to push further. With a look, she told him so.

"Such a standardized protocol, Mr. Jefferson," he therefore added, "works flawlessly in both practice and theory. Indeed, the great English experimentalist, Sir Henry Cavendish, effectively exploits the discipline for each of these purposes. He investigates with precision the discernible, very provable properties of physical objects, but also employs the exact principles to theorize the never provable, thereby enabling him among other things, to surmise the total weight of the Earth itself."

"What?" barked the bishop, unbelieving this strange statement. "Why would he do that, what function could it possibly serve? Such information is meaningless."

"Precisely," proclaimed Ward, "that's the whole idea, sir. Understand it's the set method that's important, independent of its use. Every pure Science such as mathematics demonstrates this principle, for it is, in itself, also totally meaningless."

"Now hold on," said Jefferson, "I use math often. It certainly has meaning. That's its function."

"Yes, but only when the discipline is applied," the woman pointed out. "After all, the process is the same, regardless. For example, what's one plus one?"

The President raised his eyebrows at this simplistic inquiry. The bishop leaned forward, awaiting his answer. Neither of them understood her thrust.

"Two, of course," Jefferson answered.

"Yes," the young woman concurred, but then she quickly wondered, "But two what, exactly?"

"Why, two anything," Madison replied.

"Yes," she said again, "or two nothing. One plus one will always equal two, it's a given. The application doesn't matter for, useful or not, either way it's a fact."

"Science is only a tool, as I've noted," Ward added. "Yet the method, rigid but surprisingly simple, permits boundless opportunities. It just needs to be used."

After this, no one spoke. The implication was clear enough. Education achieved without imposed truth stood apart, and was a check against blind assumption.

"Thus," at last reasoned the bishop, "under such a stratagem, the inherent flaws of History would not be repeated, and knowledge gleaned by it would be built from the bottom up, so to speak, no longer dictated from above."

"Yes, that is the beauty of the method," the redhead concurred. "The inherent advantages are self-evident. Results would then be limited only by application."

"Jamie, that's precisely the point I've been trying to make," said Jefferson, almost pleading. "Furthermore, I don't reject the Almighty, nor need the students. They should embrace Him in a church, that's all, not in Virginia's new university."

"Render unto Caesar, as it were," observed Madison, still ruminating. He began to tap his long fingers on the table, the tips dancing up and down in rapid succession. From long experience, Jefferson deduced this action a positive sign.

At last the bishop stood and crossed to his oldest friend.

"I'm afraid that I cannot agree," he stated, looking glum. Then he indicated the bottle resting before the President. "At least," he added, "without more claret."

Jefferson's eyes filled with tears but, composing himself, this passed. He then also stood, facing his dearest companion since childhood. They embraced.

A new toast was then proposed.

Later, the time travelers were sitting in the buckboard, once more clomping over the cobblestones.

"Would he not have convinced him on his own?" she asked.

"Perhaps," the tall man answered. "Yet now the precedent will be firmly set. This example will become the norm, begetting perpetual changes to the future."

She only nodded, knowing it was so.

"You were superb," he informed her. "Quite lucid, and you never lost your head. Still, as a matter of course, we need to evaluate the mission in detail."

Again she nodded, once more knowing it was so.

Back at the mansion, the two Virginian's were yet marveling over the newly arrived specimens, but at last they had successfully corroborated the inventory. It was late, but neither was fatigued by the effort. Quite the contrary.

"Do you continue to edit your own Bible?" Jamie wondered. "Still working away, snipping out the parts with which you disagree? Is there any Old Testament left?"

Tommy laughed aloud, for it was true. His project was long term, and he'd never give it up. Also, the older Testament was indeed the most heavily altered.

"Don't worry," the President tried to reassure him. "I'm being very scientific in my scrutiny. So naturally, this new version will be quite meaningless."

"Thank God for that," rejoiced the bishop.

His companion easily concurred with this sentiment. Now he had only one regret. The remarkable redheaded woman had failed to view any of his wonderful renderings.

Yet, unknown to him, she had a copy of each one on file.

7
Dinner with the Doge
Or
Stagnation vs. Directional Change

"It's time, Hal," said the disembodied voice, seemingly uttered from nowhere. Yet it was familiar, and this was somehow comforting. Then, the formerly sleeping man opened his eyes, suddenly remembering who he was.

"Already?" he asked, still prone but now blinking a few times in vain hopes of focusing on something tangible in the dim room, which was currently lit only by a small corner fireplace and a few strategically dispersed candles.

"Look, you oaf, it's not yet sunrise," Hal then observed, casting a glance through the darkened window. Always grumpy after awakening, he next added, "I see no one here. Have they come to attend us, are they outside?"

"No," calmly answered the other, while holding forth a large tankard of steaming, heavily spiced wine. "But soon enough. The uncooperative wind has finally arrived."

This got the attention of the man in the bed. He tried to sit up a few times, but these were only hasty and futile attempts. Being quite corpulent, he extended his beefy arm, wishing assistance.

"To our advantage, or theirs?" he inquired.

"Theirs, I'm afraid," uttered the standing man. And then, he added, "You know what you must do, Hal. It must be done quickly, and you know this, also."

Hal was busy downing his tankard while these words were being spoken. This day he would need his wits about him and the warm wine would surely help. Plus, he always loved warmed, spicy wine in the morning.

"Delightful," he said, while wiping his mouth with his sleeve. Next, holding out the empty cup, he sighed and belched. The standing man, using a deep ladle, then refilled it from a copper vessel hanging in the fireplace.

"I will not make peace with the French," suddenly barked the seated man, who still disheveled was nevertheless the current King of England. "They are in my waters, and I won't have it. I must deal with them, and will."

The standing man, who held the pissing pot, now also sighed.

"And they call me a fool," he said.

Once the King was well toileted and suitably attired, which took some time to accomplish, footsteps were heard approaching in the hall. It was now well past dawn. The two occupants of the starkly furnished, yet best available room in the small fortress, were now standing abreast, waiting.

Three loud knocks on the door followed, whereupon the royal sentry outside opened it to reveal half a dozen well dressed gentlemen standing in the corridor.

"My Liege," said the Constable of Southsea Castle, bowing with great deference. The men surrounding him quickly did likewise. "I trust Your Majesty slept well even given our crude accommodations," he added.

The King, by chance visiting nearby Portsmouth when informed of the newly arrived French fleet, had the day before invested the diminutive outpost, one of many fortifications built to protect the large northern estuary off the Isle of Wight. The small castle's crenulated wall would give a spectacular, unobstructed view of events and Henry, after decades of spending good money on his navy, wanted to see the result of this royal largesse. He therefore anticipated a good show.

"My Lords," he decreed, "I shall savor sweet sleep only when England is safe. Tell me of the wind. It now favors the enemy?"

"It does, Your Majesty," answered the realm's Secretary of State, William Paget, who stood beside the castle's Constable. "The Lord High Admiral Russel, now observing from the wall above, has already dispatched some number of rowbarges, the only craft we currently possess that will advance without sail, to meet several French galleys that are currently probing our line. And yet, my Lord Admiral believes the wind may soon turn, and to our advantage, or so he says."

To this declaration, the unimpressed King only grunted. Then he stepped forward, toward the men who all stepped back at his advance. But at the doorway he turned, once more looking to his Royal Jester, William Sommers.

"And what will you do today, Billy?" he asked the very tall man.

"I shall travel to Venice, Hal," calmly answered his hardworking fool, "twenty-five years hence, to sup with the Doge."

The men in the hallway all laughed at this response, but His Majesty did not. He knew this unique person as no one else did. King Henry was well aware that if he truly wished to undertake such a sojourn he certainly could.

This seemingly simple servant, the Sovereign understood, was in reality a time traveler.

"You still have an option," added the determined jester, his thin face devoid of emotion.

Henry's vividly dark, pinched and beady eyes met those of the tall man, looking deeply into them, searching but not finding any further meaning hidden there.

"You are a fool," answered the King, but smiling as he spoke.

The day, bright and beautiful, turned long with little real action attached, at first. The wind, ever changing was always slight, and neither side did more than maneuver at some distance from one another. The rowbarges, never coming close enough, did not engage the enemy, who lacking propulsion simply failed to arrive.

Upon the parapet, the King and his advisors spent the opportunity eating and drinking, and talking of the coming confrontation. Considering the unique nature of the still unfolding situation, royal functionaries were kept to a minimum but those on hand milled about ready for service, if need be. Many livered attendants were of course near by, as they were always present in abundant numbers about the King's person.

There was much speculation by everyone as to what would occur once the fleets engaged, for the indecisive wind often increased but always departed, and this left plenty of time to while away whilst discussing the subject.

The King's still nascent navy was tiny, much smaller than the mighty French fleet, but being from an island nation his seamen, unlike hers, were real sailors. Other major European powers such as France or Spain used their fleets mainly for transporting troops and equipment to fight on land, but England's ships fought at sea, and well understood its advantages. And, the navy's two principal warships were now present in the Solent, the expansive waterway betwixt the Isle of Wight and England's southern coast.

Portsea Island stood midway on the estuary, and Southsea Castle was located at its point. The sweeping vantage presented between the fort's crenels was indeed panoramic. By noon, the stagnated wind again picked up.

"How many French ships?" demanded the King, sensing at last a change in the stalemated status quo. He stood at the wall, squinting in the distance. "More than me, that's easy to see," he added, in a regal but sour tone.

"At least two hundred, Your Majesty," answered Henry's Lord High Admiral, who was standing nearby at the nearest break in the masonry. "We have but eighty or so. Several of yours, however, are more massive," he quickly added.

This statement referred to England's two largest ocean-going craft, both of them interesting ships, and for several reasons.

First, they were designed and constructed specifically for warfare at sea, a unique circumstance given the times. Other ships of war, in England and elsewhere were always converted merchantmen, or were built by altering the well-established designs of ocean-going commercial vessels. Yet, by intention these two specimens were far superior craft, being not merely sturdy transporters of men and arms, but huge, coordinated and highly mobile, total weapon systems in themselves.

Second, after seeing long years of heavy action in two separate and brutal wars against two different but equally stubborn French kings, both ships had been successfully and painstakingly retrofitted with the latest technological innovations. These included sealing gunports amid multiple decks that employed bronze and iron cannon and demi-cannon of various sizes. Most guns were now also breech-loaded, and this innovative time saving advancement granted much inherent advantage.

These novel arrangements permitted for the first time in nautical history the use of the broadside, a practice whereby all arms a ship possessed, port or starboard, or even both if need be, could be fired simultaneously.

The development would quite alter standard naval tactics, by setting in place unfolding changes in strategy becoming preeminent for hundreds of years.

The larger of the two great ships, the Mary Rose, was literally bristling with guns, for a new complement of cannon had been installed amidships upon an added tier between the castles, which were the higher decks on either end of the carrack-style vessel. These opposing rows of artillery naturally made the gigantic boat much heavier and so increased her displacement, which meant that she sat lower in the sea. In fact, now fully manned and abundantly provisioned, her first line of gunports rode only three feet above the waterline, a detail of some importance.

"What's happening?" barked the impatient King.

His chief functionaries, who were scattered about the edge of the parapet, had no suitable response to this royal inquiry. None of them knew. Still, the King could not be kept waiting, so the Lord Admiral was soon compelled to answer.

"It appears, Your Majesty," he admitted, "the unimpressive winds have once more died."

"Blast it," screamed Henry, "blast it to Hades."

He turned to retake his appointed seat, a heavy chair in the near distance placed under a colorful canopy, beside an equally heavy table that bore much food and libation, but midway there the King changed his mind.

Exercising the royal prerogative, he instead stomped off, announcing over his shoulder, "My Lords, I'm to my accommodations to rest my leg. Send word once something occurs. Until then, I'm not to be disturbed."

"Majesty," and "Sire," and such were uttered by all present. Each of them bowed toward the retreating regal presence. Two gentlemen, the Constable and his Lieutenant, followed the King in order to assure his safe transit.

The hard working fool was dutifully waiting to tend his Sovereign's acute affliction, something he'd done many times before. The King of England had a large, pungent ulcer on his upper thigh, which for years had stubbornly refused to mend. The ever-oozing wound was washed and redressed several times daily, a protocol of long standing that thus far had failed to achieve any suitable, permanent solution.

"Well, Billy boy, how was your visit?" asked the Monarch, once his enormous leg, newly exposed, was propped across a crude wooden stool. "Have a good dinner out of your excursion, did you? Something tasty I trust, for all of your trouble."

"It was a dismal failure," the jester replied flatly, "the Doge is as hardheaded as you, I fear. But, I've another invitation a week hence that will, from my point of view, take place later today, just after we're done here. Of course, from your reference, it won't happen for another twenty-five years."

He was dabbing thick green pus from Henry's thigh as he spoke. This ministration, as those that would follow was deliberate, yet slowly and gently delivered. Still, the time traveler knew such action was useless in the long term.

The royal lesion would never heal.

"What do you wish from him?" inquired the King, referring to the Doge. After all, international intrigue was Henry's life's blood. He was highly interested, for His Majesty always relished political machinations and stratagem of any kind.

"He has to stop warring with the Sultan," answered the nursing man, "as you must with the French. The time is ripe, and Europe should now turn its eyes westward, as I've told you. Your beautiful sailing ships, and those of other European powers will permit this occurrence, but only when peace comes."

"Why grant accommodation when I can win?" asked the King.

"But will you win?" countered the fool. "The French are more numerous, and the uncooperative weather remains fickle. Yet, you still have time to alter things."

"How so?" inquired Henry.

The patient jester then began to wash the King's open wound, a gaping and most grisly one. The unforgiving ulcer was deeply buried within the noble but flabby flesh. Periodically, the upper layer of skin did mostly recover but, in each instance, it was only a matter of time before the gash once more erupted, and ever with a nasty, highly odiferous vengeance.

"My Lord Brandon, as we speak, is being rowed ashore," explained his fool. "He's been conferring with Admiral Dudley aboard his flagship, the Great Harry. The finalized order of attack has now been dispersed to the fleet, but the languid wind still gives you leave to countermand this proposed action."

Charles Brandon, the first Duke of Suffolk, was Henry's oldest friend, his closest advisor, and his former brother-in-law. Years ago, he had married the King's now dead sister, Mary Tudor. The Mary Rose was named for her.

John Dudley, currently Viscount Lisle, was in overall command of the assembled fleet. One day in the not too distant future, Lord Dudley would be invested the first Duke of Northumberland. On another day further still, Henry's oldest daughter, who was also named Mary, would execute him, after he'd tried but failed to install as Queen his son's most docile wife, the very plain and overly pitiful Lady Jane Grey.

Without hesitation Henry decreed, "No, I will see this through, my dear Billy. I've no other course open to me. I cannot make peace at such a disadvantage."

The nurse began to rewrap the wound but Henry waved him off. His Majesty was most agitated. True, this was his normal demeanor, but now more so.

"Leave it," he mumbled in a distracted fashion, and then in a louder voice he commanded, "Let it breathe for a while."

The jester then leaned back and sat on the floor before the King. For a moment neither man spoke. Then Henry, still wishing answers, continued his scrutiny.

"Tell me of the Doge," he requested. "Why does he not comply with your wishes? What stops him from making peace?"

The tall man rearranged himself, by wrapping his long arms around his longer legs, after pulling his knees up under his chin.

"Venice will lose Cyprus in the treaty, her last Mediterranean island, a heavy price for such a proud people," answered the sitting man. "Yet he must accept this difficult condition, and will. As you do, he just needs persuading."

The King of England laughed aloud at this proclamation. No one ever told him what to do, or lasted long after such an affront. No one but his fool, that is.

"And how will you change him?" then asked Henry.

"I shall take a different dinner guest with me," was the answer. "The one I took this morning was unimpressive, as I've said. Still, given that the groundwork is now sufficiently laid, my new company should nicely do the trick."

Henry, adjusting his great bulk in the chair, then grunted.

"Whom did you take?" he wondered.

"I thought the Doge needed a framework," was the reply, "a tangible yet palatable argument for making peace with the dreaded Turk, the horrid infidel. For this reason, I took the much revered fourth century Bishop of Hippo, for he has swayed millions having such concerns. Yet, the Doge was unmoved."

"What's that you say?" demanded the now startled King, with his earlier malaise quite vanished. "Are you telling me that you personally conveyed Saint Augustine to dinner with the Doge of Venice? You accompanied Saint Augustine himself?"

"The very same," was the response, "as the good bishop was expert at supplying cogent rationale for unlikely circumstance."

Henry had a great belly laugh at this, cackling, "What a rogue you are, Billy. You never cease to amaze me. Tell me everything."

The jester stood, now seeing this would take some time. He fetched the King a flagon of wine and a hard roll, handing them over. Then, again, he sat.

"You must know the context," he lectured. "Augustine was more than a mere theologian. The principles he espoused have since framed your society, establishing the basic rules of civilization for the last twelve hundred years."

At this, the King grunted once more, for usually he didn't like theologians of any stripe. English ones were bad enough, and the current Pope was in league with his sworn enemy, the French. The Spanish, while also loathing them were Catholic, so an alliance with Spain was not a viable option.

"Bishop Augustine lived," the lecture continued, "while Rome's imperial power crumbled, the set decrees falling away. By this time, the population was Christian but barely so, and any fresh rules were yet to be firmly recognized. But now, in every locale new Christian princes wished to war with other Christian princes, a troubling obstacle if you're a diligent churchman busy building a religion based on peace and love."

"I see it," announced the marveling King. "You speak of the Doctrine of Just War, the moral reasoning behind why Christians may fight. Honor, and so forth."

"Yes, but even more," countered the fool. "Having such new stipulations gave Europe the time it needed to coalesce, to rebuild intuitions, to set things in place. Now, after more than a thousand years this has slowly happened, and the time has come to move on, as I've explained to you before, Hal."

"I am no Doge," snapped Henry, disliking the implication. "I'm a King, not a functionary of some committee of state. I am my country, Billy, I am England."

This pompous pronouncement caused the fool to laugh aloud.

"You?" he replied. "Why Hal, you're just a single link in the long chain of history, and a very lengthy procession that is, too. You may control this petty kingdom but not events in general, that's quite beyond your allotted purview."

"What?" screamed the King, instantly livid. "You push your limits, man. This line is not humorous, and you overstep your bounds at your own peril."

The jester, leaning back, didn't answer this outburst. He knew the raging tempest would soon pass. He knew this stubborn man very well, much better than did even the first Duke of Suffolk, the King's oldest friend, Charles Brandon.

"See the bigger picture, Hal," he finally said. "There have been Doges in Venice for over eight hundred years, with many more yet to come. Your esteemed family, ever-glorious now, has ruled England for barely two generations."

After this stiff truism, Henry threw his hard roll to the floor in disgust, but then he thought the better of it. Tantrums solved nothing. He knew this to be factual, for he employed them often and they never worked.

And also, he was hungry again.

"My point," emphasized the fool, "is the rigid framework set by Augustine is now no longer sufficient. Another direction is needed, a new way of looking at things, for knowledge has been sanctioned, only dictated from above. But, no more."

"What does that mean?" grumbled Henry, not following.

"Twelve hundred years ago," said the jester, "Augustine stated knowledge of any kind was a thing given only by God. Ergo, to know anything at all was a gift from God. Knowledge gained without God's grace then became heretical."

This comment made His Majesty smile. Generally, the King favored a good heretic. After all, he was the biggest one yet.

"This arrangement, while providing local stability had its limits," added his fool, "for people are ever curious and naturally inquisitive, and any such restriction is always stifling. So, to ease these well-placed concerns, three hundred years ago the enlightened Thomas Aquinas decreed that God-given knowledge really comes in two forms. These are understandings which you can discover on your own, by God's grace, and that which is known only to Him, granted through divine revelation."

"Yes," declared Henry, "and what's wrong with that? It makes good sense. The Darker Ages are long in the past, and we have much new knowledge now, as my fearsome ships will soon demonstrate to the French fleet."

"Are they over?" asked the jester, trying once more to make the elusive connection. "How, when knowledge still remains tangible in itself, a real thing at which you may chisel away as some sculptor would, dribbling off random pieces, as it were? No, Hal, adherence to such a stilted outlook has inherent disadvantages that are no longer acceptable."

"But what other way is there?" asked the baffled ruler.

The patient time traveler began to rewrap Henry's leg.

"Make peace with the French," was his answer, "and find out."

It was now late afternoon, and the wind came up in earnest. The Sovereign, below with his companion, was duly informed. Presently he was upon the rampart.

"What news, My Lords?" the King, now wearing clean leggings, asked of his retinue, after making his slow but regal transition to the wall above the broad estuary.

"The wind is up, Henry," answered the newly arrived Duke of Suffolk, who then affectionately embraced his oldest friend. This particular personage solely possessed such a uniquely granted privilege, and so he often shunned the standard convention of great deference to the royal station and regularly addressed the King by name. "Soon, Vice Admiral Carew will advance with his flagship, the Mary Rose," the nobleman added, thinking of his long dead wife, the King's once beautiful sister.

"She moves, Your Majesty," announced Lord Admiral Russel, who was, as his title indicated, head of the entire English navy.

"Magnificent," declared the Constable of Southsea Castle.

Everyone looked to the huge ship floating gracefully in the near distance, her sails already fully deployed and gently filling with air.

"And what will happen now?" asked the eager Monarch.

"She will soon turn and lead the line of attack," answered Suffolk, as if it were only a foregone conclusion, which it was.

Aboard the Mary Rose, the very command was being given.

"Prepare to bring her about," the Vice Admiral calmly said to an aide, and quickly the order was shouted to runners who would disperse it throughout the crew. "Close all starboard gunports," he added next. This most critical instruction was passed on as well, yet it somehow failed to reach the two lowest decks, and that salient fact had both immediate and dire consequences.

Soon the giant ship began to slowly turn. Next, a robust gust of wind swept across the vessel, snapping taunt her full complement of sail. Then the impressive Mary Rose, the very pinnacle of current nautical innovation and design, was herself broadsided.

Already riding deeply in the water, she now listed just enough for the sea to rush in through the still open gunports along her lower tier of starboard artillery. This swiftly pulled her further down, which shifted everything stowed aboard towards the rapidly increasing tilt of the ship. The lashing ropes that bound the heavy guns stationed opposite soon gave way under the tremendous strain and ripped apart, sending the cannon, and their great weight crashing across the distance and into the now flooding compartments above the great vessel's main hold.

This cavity was vast, the deepest section of the Mary Rose, an immense, already fully packed storage chamber, now breeched and filling with water, as well.

The second tier of open gunports was swamped in less than one minute, and the same unabated process then repeated, sharply increasing the ever-growing angle of list.

Onboard was complete chaos. The massive ship was quickly, totally overwhelmed and sucked under. Because the enemy still used the older tactics of boarding a vessel for hand-to-hand combat, heavy webbing had been strung across the upper decks to repel such an onslaught, and the hapless sailors and soldiers stationed on these various levels were all trapped within the substantial ropes, like fish in a net.

"My God," gasped the Lord High Admiral. It was all that needed to be said. Everyone else was too stunned to speak.

Henry simply stood with his royal mouth hanging open.

Soon, all that could be seen of the once impressive ship was her topmost sails, tilted at a sixty-degree angle for, hitting bottom, the doomed vessel had settled into the deep mud, hidden but just awaiting beneath the murky water. All manner of items were now floating about, somehow escaping the netting. Only the men clinging to the upper rigging survived the calamity, less than forty of well over four hundred total aboard.

Most of the casualties occurred below. Many died there before the boat sank, crushed by items loosened in the dramatic shifting involved, but to a man, the others were swallowed alive. Those on the upper decks, all ensnared by the nets, each drowned while viewing the elusive surface in the near distance above them.

Then the feckless wind, the last of the waning day also died, bringing to an end the so-called Battle of the Solent. The French, thinking better of the entire campaign, soon withdrew their fleet. Needless to say, the engagement was inconclusive.

Henry also withdrew, and without comment to anyone moved to his room where the fool was awaiting him. No one present spoke as the King exited, being prompted by a quickly raised hand of the Duke of Suffolk, an action that silenced them. But they all deeply bowed as His Majesty slowly made his passage.

"Well, Billy boy, you've taught me an unkind lesson today," hissed the proud but now outmaneuvered Monarch. "Yes, you've done me harshly this time. Why?"

King Henry stood defiantly before the taller man, jutting his noble jaw and holding his much-recognized stiffened stance, portrayed so well in many an official portrait.

"The choice was yours," countered the fool, "I caused no change. You failed to alter something, and that had consequences. Now you must carry on, Hal."

Henry could not speak. He tried, but he only sputtered, his usual pale completion currently a flaming red. At last, giving up the effort, he turned and sat.

For a moment, nothing happened. The fool waited, as he always did. The King brooded, as he often did.

Henry was defeated, and he knew it. He also knew he didn't like being beaten. But Billy was right, of course, he always was.

The King of England would have to move on.

"Yes," he said at last, "you did warn me, that is true enough."

The jester offered food and wine, but Henry, still most distracted, didn't notice the effort.

"Well," he finally said, almost spitting the words, "at least tell me of your trip to the Doge. Were you successful? Has he now also agreed to do your damn bidding?"

"He has, Hal," was the answer, given while ignoring the royal sarcasm. "My latest dinner guest convinced him, as I'd hoped he would. Now, at long last a new enlightenment will begin, a totally different way of looking at things."

Henry grunted. His Majesty would see to it that some things were soon looked into, that's for sure. Yes, change was coming, and in more ways that one.

He began to formulate a plan, but almost immediately gave it up. He had people for that. He'd wait and rule on what they suggested, employing his standard procedure.

"Tell me of your encounter with the Doge," he instead demanded, wishing to speak of other matters. "Who did you convey this time? Why was he effective?"

"I took an Englishman, actually," the time traveler replied. "He won't be born for another sixteen years, but he was middle aged when we arrived. A most interesting gentleman, for his bold ideas indeed changed everything."

"I see," stated Henry, "but how so?"

"It's all a matter of perception," the fool calmly explained. "How does anyone judge what truly is? Must they blindly follow what's come before, believing something only because others previous have, or do they instead think in another way, a better way, with new eyes that can see new things?"

"Speak plainly," advised the weary King, "what do you mean?"

"In the old scheme, all truth was known but hidden," he related. "That will now change. Soon, nothing will be taken for granted, and all knowledge will thus be built only by what is shown to be factual, a great distinction."

"I don't follow," said Henry, "what matters this distinction?"

The jester again offered food and drink, and this time Henry, now much calmer, accepted.

"Again, it's perception," the fool continued. "Knowledge is not a given thing that's dispersed, but an unknown thing that's discovered. And this new outlook, this simple difference will lead to all kind of changes in the future."

Here he paused, to give the King time to absorb this input.

"An Englishman, you say?" asked Henry, after his absorption was completed. "Who is he, or rather, who shall he be? A philosopher of some description?"

"Not exactly," was the answer, "he's a lawyer, or will be one."

"Oh dear," mused the King. He despised all lawyers, and everyone knew it. In his regal opinion, they were as bad as churchmen, maybe worse.

"His friends will be the philosophers, natural philosophers they will soon label themselves," informed the fool. "Yet these thinkers will have no firm foundation, no standard set of rules agreed to by all. He changes this, by supplying them a method of inquiry, a universally acceptable system to be known as Science."

"This Science," reasoned the King, "this system of simple distinction, is so important? Why? What exactly will it do?"

"Humans now have ocean-going craft," the other man pointed out, "and the world will soon be cracked open by them. This widely opened world will also have Science, as well. Great change is therefore inevitable, Hal, but it's only possible now because the time is right and the proper conditions are finally present."

After a moment, having made the connection, Henry said, "I understand now," then quickly he asked, "Who is this Englishman that changes everything so?"

"His name is Bacon," was the answer, "Francis Bacon."

Henry roared at this, his bilious body jiggling with laughter.

"Wonderful," he cried, "I've always loved pork."

"You've always loved everything, Hal, that's your problem," countered the jester, as he refilled Henry's cup of wine.

"So tell me," urged the King, "what will happen hence?"

"Europe will turn now westward, as I've said, begetting world-wide influence," the all-knowing man revealed. "In a hundred years, an Irishman named Boyle will decipher mysteries from the very air we breathe, and in two hundred a man from the new world named Franklin will pull power from lightning. A hundred years after that, a Frenchman named Pasteur will prove beyond all doubt that things too small to be seen can affect life itself, a tremendous discovery leading to much change."

"And what of England?" next asked Henry.

"Because of you," said Billy, "England will be strong. Her navy will become great. It shall rule the waves for hundreds of years."

This pleasant news pleased Henry greatly, but only because he'd now made the bigger connection. The future was his to command. He wouldn't let it down.

He stood and crossed to the door, then jerked it open.

The crowded hallway was full of his startled functionaries and favorites. Some men were standing, while others were sitting on heavy benches against either wall. No matter their placement, all were awaiting the King's pleasure.

"Charles," he barked, and the Duke of Suffolk dutifully stood. "I shall have peace with France," Henry announced. Suffolk only nodded, and then sat as before.

"Your Majesty," interjected Lord Paget, who'd jumped up at the King's sudden appearance. As England's Secretary of State, this lofty bureaucrat would have to negotiate any treaty with the French invaders, and he didn't relish doing so under the current tactical conditions. Yet Henry was unconcerned with that aspect.

"I will have my peace with France," screamed the monarch, and Paget also nodded and sat.

Then Henry, ever intent on hasty retreat, began to turn from the room's threshold but, exercising his royal prerogative, he first commanded, "And, bring pork for dinner."

Then he slammed the door.

His fool now held the washbasin, a towel draped over his arm.

Sleep came late that night for the eighth English King crowned Henry. He was abed, but thinking. His Majesty was leaving on the morrow, to continue his recent, interrupted progress through the south of his realm, but he was troubled and his active mind refused to cease its unrelenting rambling.

"Billy," he called out softly.

"Yes, Hal," came the answer from the darkness, "I'm here."

"When the world is new," began the royal pondering, "will they know what I did? Will anyone care that I made peace with the French? Will they even remember me at all?"

This whispered inquiry caused the jester to laugh aloud.

"And they call me a fool," the time traveler said.

8
The Crazy Old Sandman
Or
General Mechanics of Warfare

The stranger in the stricken city currently found himself pressed for time, a most uncommon occurrence. The rushing man usually held more than enough of that elusive commodity for he was, in fact, a time traveler. As a rule, his agenda was fixed and unchanging, and normally it flowed in a flawless fashion.

Not today.

No, on this occasion his vaulted calculations were undeniably off. Given the present mission's parameters, this was ironic as well as inconvenient. The subject of this operation was the greatest mathematical mind the world had yet produced.

Still, the stranger was running late and time was of the essence.

He did know that the old man he sought had to be nearby, for his general whereabouts on this particular day were well known to history. Yet, the city was large, and given its wall was now breached, many frightened citizens were crowding the narrow streets, intent on seeking a safe haven. There was none.

Nevertheless, the determined stranger, who was taller by a head compared to the populace, hadn't accounted for the mass of struggling humanity he'd come upon, and wading through it was setting him behind schedule.

The standing confrontation had been under way for nearly two years now, an unheard of circumstance given the combatants involved. The attacking Legions consisted of battle-hardened troops well versed in siege craft and a walled city, as a rule, was no long-term obstacle for them to face. The old man was though, as they had all quickly learned.

The Roman commander was especially impressed. Marcus Claudius Marcellus had already subdued the rest of the large island, filling his time while awaiting the city's slow starvation, but this strategy had failed to deliver capitulation. However, always proficient, he was a most observant man, and lately this crafty warrior had noticed a hidden weakness in the wall.

Also, Hannibal was now standing in the wings, so to speak, so Marcellus was truly an impatient General with more battles left to fight. Still, he needed Sicily first. Of course, he'd get it, but he wanted the old man holed up in Syracuse, as well.

For this reason, the night before he had issued the order.

"He must be taken alive," he stressed to his second in command. "This old legend is a wonder, a human enigma. At all costs, he must not be killed."

"Sir," protested his second, "that may not be possible. The city will be in chaos. Things happen quickly, and butchering Legionnaires don't stop to think."

Marcellus looked up at this statement, ready to bark his disagreement. Yet, seeing his junior's earnest, professional demeanor, he didn't. He took instead another approach, employing a different strategy altogether.

"We must know what he knows," he said slowly, for emphasis. "You weren't here then, you didn't see it. We were attacked before we even landed, by several monstrosities he'd created, weapons completely unknown to man."

His second knew this. Everyone did. The innovative contraptions were now famous throughout the Empire.

The first were especially hideous, gigantic towers having movable arms containing huge hooks. These expertly plucked several galleys from the sea itself, hurling them into other ships. It was a terrifying welcome that took many lives.

Next came the devastating fire, delivered by the sun's rays which were employed by several banks of polished mirrors most skillfully directed at the wooden ships and their fabric sails. More time and good Legionnaires lost before the army, by sheer weight of numbers had landed and forced the installations at heavy loss. And all of this grisly action occurred before the formal campaign had even started in earnest.

Two years on land had not altered the stagnated situation. Attacks continued, and always by previously unknown means used to the deadliest of effect. Yes, the old man in the city was a sly one, no doubting that undisputed fact.

Yet this changed nothing. Attacking soldiers were not nursemaids, and how could one man in thousands be assured, given the true aim was taking the ancient metropolis? The second saw no sense in such an order.

"Sir," he said again, trying harder to press his case, "we don't know where he is, or even what he looks like. With his involvement to date, I'd think a bounty on his head would be the more proper thing. After all, he's the enemy, and I'd gladly exterminate him myself if I only knew who he was."

This caused General Marcellus to laugh. He crossed to his comrade and placed his hand on the man's shoulder. Next he spoke as a mentor, an expert in killing.

"Egypt was strong," he lectured him, "for she had fine chariots while her enemies did not. Yet they first acquired horses from their adversaries, and now Hannibal has elephants. The victory is ever in the new, and the winning army will always use the latest innovation, it must to survive or its enemies will do so first."

Marcellus, as a rule, knew a few things about winning. The man never lost in either battle or politics, quite the opposite. He'd already been Consul three times, an unheard of thing for a commoner, and he'd hold the vaulted office twice more.

As for the military side, the great warrior had risen from nothing without benefit of family connections or influential friends conveniently placed in upper level politics. This General had seemingly advanced on merit alone and he was very good at liquidating the enemy, and also for arranging vast numbers of others to do so. Undefeated in any previous endeavor, Marcus Claudius Marcellus could well afford to be magnanimous now.

He patted his second's armored shoulder, affectionately as a concerned and loving father would do.

"See the bigger picture," he said softly. "This is a great gift just awaiting the taking, and we should pluck it. Who knows what else he could come up with, given time?"

His second, a competent man, made the proper connection. The old one was more than just a costly inconvenience. He was a valuable military commodity.

Still, this experienced soldier knew the order itself would mean nothing once the real fighting started.

The conflagration was well under way when at last the stranger reached the proper district in Syracuse, yet it raged near the far wall, still at some distance. Before dawn, a small detachment of elite troops using a blind spot had crept over and succeeded in opening an isolated, barricaded gate. This hotly contested entry was by definition a bottleneck, but it was only a matter of time before the Romans broke through en masse.

He scanned the area, normally a pleasant square that was now full of screaming citizens bent on retreating toward the inner city. The action would do them no good in the long run. This day Syracuse would see much slaughter, the heavy price paid for siding with Carthage, the Empire's current enemy of choice.

"Where's the Master?" the stranger asked a running boy he'd recognized and snagged from the crowd. "The mathematician, the wise one? He lives near."

"The crazy old man who scribbles pictures in the sand?" snapped the frightened boy. He was indignant at being stopped. He shook himself free.

"Behind the fountain," he screamed before scampering off.

The stranger made his way over passing through the now thinning crowd. Indeed, the old man, hidden from view and oblivious to the unfolding action around him, was sitting and leaning against the short wall of the fountain. He held a long stick in his hand and was looking down at many figures, ovals and lines, that he had drawn in the sand.

"Master," said the stranger, "we must make haste. The time is nigh for the wall is finally breached, the city soon to be overrun with Legionnaires. They'll be looking for you and, as I've explained, there will be no safety here."

The old man did not answer. He was engrossed by his symbols, making incisive connections that others would not reconstruct for over a thousand years. So great was his vast concentration that he was quite unaware of anything else around him.

"Master, please," begged the harried stranger in a louder voice, and this time the old man turned to look up at him.

"Oh," he observed, "it's you again. Back as you said you'd be, I see. What's that you mentioned, the wall is truly breached?"

The stranger only nodded.

"Well, that's it, I suppose," the mathematician flatly stated. "I've done what I could. These Romans are most persistent."

By now the square was deserted, but the sounds of combat were getting closer, with screams and the din of clashing weaponry filling the nearby streets.

"We must hurry," the stranger reiterated.

The old man sighed but didn't move beyond looking once more to the symbols in the sand before him.

"No," he said, "I'm close now. And I must know. If time is short then I will use it well, by making my final connection while I can."

The time traveler was the now the one who sighed. He knew further argument was moot. No one, not even he, could tell the great Archimedes of Syracuse what to do.

Next, a few defenders ran by the fountain, retreating deeper into the city. The stranger turned and walked into the center of the square. He didn't wait long.

A dozen Legionnaires appeared, bloody, with weapons drawn. The stranger raised his arms. The Romans, constantly looking to each other, advanced slowly.

"Archimedes is here," announced the tall man in a strong voice. "He wishes to surrender, and won't resist. By order of General Marcellus himself, he's to be taken alive."

By this time, other Romans were swarming in like ants to sweet honey, flooding the square. Most, however, kept moving, passing the unfolding situation. The original contingent now surrounded the stranger, effectively sealing him off.

A Centurion, identified by the plume of his helmet, looked to the ancient, still recumbent figure behind the fountain.

"Are you sure?" he asked the taller man. "Many swine would gladly say anything to stave off their miserable fate. I've no moment to waste, is this true?"

The stranger, resigned, only nodded. The Centurion then grunted and walked over. Time would tell, they both knew.

"Are you Archimedes?" he snarled. There was no answer as the old man was once more absorbed in his labor. "Are you Archimedes of Syracuse?" then screamed the exacerbated warrior, but again there was no response.

He stepped forward and poked the seated man with his weapon. This was too much for the genius. He'd had enough.

"You're standing on my circles," he cried out in despair, dismayed by the rude action.

Now the Centurion didn't hesitate. There was more killing to be had this day, and he and his men wanted their fair share of the butchering. Without thinking twice, he dispatched the old man with one blow of his sword.

"Forward boys," he shouted. They all ran off, joining the increasing throng of invading Romans. Then the Centurion remembered the stranger, and he turned to confront him.

Yet, he was no longer there.

At this time, General Marcellus was outside the now burning city, being kept abreast of the unfolding action by frequent dispatches born by unending runners. He had just mounted his horse. A rider approached and pulled up beside him.

"It's done," he said to the General, who nodded at the message. They both trotted off, each ruminating the consequences of the finalized event. Soon Marcellus spoke.

"He had to die," the warrior asked, "there was no other way?"

"None," said the time traveler, now dressed in Roman garb. "It had to be thus for the world needs time, as I've explained. Events will change but at a pace, and he would have set things too far ahead of the proper schedule, I'm afraid."

But the crafty stranger had again arranged things to place Marcellus in a good light, just as he'd said he would. History would judge the General innocent of involvement in the terrible deed. History would be wrong in this case, of course.

"Archimedes was more than just a very clever man," explained the stranger. "He wasn't only a great mathematician, or a superb engineer. He was a true visionary."

Marcellus nodded, being well aware that his companion would know. His enormous powers lay beyond normal understanding. The General knew this for the unique man had secretly aided his career advancement on many occasions in the past, and this added assistance had always been most effective, with Marcellus ever pleased by the positive outcome.

"What now," he asked, "when will I see you again?"

"Hannibal awaits," was the answer, cheerfully given, "and your future fame is assured, never fear."

Marcellus relished the thought of this, but he wanted details. The Roman turned to inquire further, but he didn't. He couldn't.

The horse trotting beside him was now without a rider.

The tall, time traveling stranger, his own mission now accomplished, had vanished.

Part Three
<u>HISTORY</u>

9
The Most Avuncular Patron
Or
The History of History

"Master," pleaded the ship's boy, "the men thirst. The sun is hot, and the jugs are temptingly close. They may soon take matters into their own hands."

The captain stood at the prow, his rigid back to those on board, looking forward into the collective future they all held.

"Each would be ill-advised to do so," he proclaimed, grunting. "The magic signs tell the numbers. Anyone who steals from me will taste the lash, not wine."

The boy had no answer to this stern declaration. It was so, and every crew member knew it. The magic signs were indeed fixed, and they always told the truth.

"Take your seat," commanded the mariner. "I will deal with the men. We arrive before nightfall as planned, never fear."

The boy, who'd felt himself duty bound to alert his master, returned to a bench at the stern of the ship. To do so he walked a center gangplank that ran along the vessel's length. On either side of this thin passageway, rows of seated, sun-bleached men two abreast were rhythmically pulling on oars.

The captain, still holding his unyielding stance, turned.

"We're close now boys," he announced, "it won't be long. Soon we will meet the wind and raise the sail. Then, all will have food and drink as we glide into port."

By now the boy had taken his place next to the only paying passenger this voyage. They were aboard a crudely constructed but sleek and highly effective shipping vessel, its hull now crammed full of wine, and usually it didn't carry any human cargo. But this strange, very tall man had been most persistent, and he had somehow persuaded the reluctant captain to accept his added presence during this particular crossing.

"What did I tell you?" he asked the boy, who only laughed in response at the statement's unspoken sentiment.

"Yes, the magic is most powerful," the strange man continued, "and tells all. The master's cargo is safe enough, for the men know the signs are always accurate. They may complain but none would chance the painful consequences."

"I often wonder how these magic signs work," the boy replied, thankful for the unexpected company this trip. "There are those who understand their hidden secrets. I wonder how they comprehend this wonderful thing."

"They are symbols," calmly answered the stranger. "Each sign means something, an exact number. And so, knowing what they indicate is the only magic involved."

This observation made the ship's boy think. Generally, he didn't like a thing he couldn't understand, not if it was something that could be figured out, at any rate. It was true that he was immature, but also inquisitive and very smart.

The youngster scanned the vessel's open hold, looking past the oaring men who were seated above. Beneath them, resting in neat, concentric rows were stacked countless, sealed amphora, all of which contained tasty wine. They were made of fire-hardened clay pressed from molds, and each held an identical shape that tightly fit together like the cells of a honeycomb, a most effective use of available shipping space.

Yet, due to the magic signs, the young boy knew that the elegantly packed jugs weren't really countless at all. Etched into a baked clay tablet about the size of a hand, the signs somehow held an exact total. Indeed, a magic inventory.

"How would one learn this powerful thing?" he asked his companion on the bench. "Who would teach it? Who could I ask if I wished to know of these signs?"

"Well," said the man, "I could arrange it, for I am patron to many boys who have learned them. They work for rulers or the merchants they control. But it takes time to become proficient, much longer than your stay in port, I'd say."

His companion, ever using his brain, now considered this. Being freeborn, he was employed by the master and not his property, so he could go where he wished. It was a good job though, always interesting, never stagnant or boring.

"I suppose a longer stay could be arranged," the boy admitted to himself, as well as the stranger.

The passenger smiled. This was exactly what he'd hoped to hear. He continued his instruction.

"There will be a young woman at the docks, several berths down," he informed the now most attentive boy. "I am her patron. She teaches the signs and she will teach you too, if you give her this and tell her that I requested that she do so."

He held out a carved stone amulet that he'd pulled from a pouch that was tied at his waist.

"This is Isis, the Ionian goddess," the stranger explained. "The woman at the dock is named Isis as well, for her mother was an Ionian slave. She'll know it's from me, for I told her I'd bring her one when I returned this trip."

"You will not speak to her?" he asked the man.

"No, not now," the stranger replied, "I have pressing business elsewhere, I'm afraid. That's why I arranged this unconventional passage. Just wait with her and I'll soon return, then we'll take you to my academy where you will easily learn the magic."

Again the boy paused to consider. This was astounding news. Yet he knew such a situation would never come to pass.

"I cannot pay," he noted with a sad tone. "I am but a poor lad. I have nothing of value to barter for such a grand service."

The stranger only smiled at this observation.

"You need not pay me now," he reassured him, "for I will be your patron as I am to her, and you can repay as she does, by teaching others in my name."

"You would do this?" the amazed youngster asked him. "Why? You don't even know me."

The stranger, again smiling, answered, "I know many things. I know you are a most intelligent boy. And I know you are motivated, and wish to learn."

"Hold off the oars," then screamed the newly contented captain, still standing at the ship's prow, "we've met the wind, at last. Man the lines. We'll have an easy time of it now."

His crew screamed in joy. They quickly stowed their oars upright by stuffing the butt ends into holes along the side rails. Then they deployed the sail.

The ship's boy, now having duties, jumped up as well and busied himself by doling out rations to the weary sailors. The stranger, still sitting, watched him. The man was most pleased, for he knew the boy would accept his proposition.

This very strange, tall man knew everything. However, this was not so surprising given his true avocation. He was, in fact, a time traveler on a mission.

At the docks, which were a bustle of activity, the boy found the lady in question just where the stranger said she'd be. She was young, only a few years older than he. She was also very pretty, something the man hadn't mentioned.

She seemed to be supervising several boys, each of whom was observing various cargo being loaded or unloaded, all while checking against signs baked into a clay tablet. At last she turned and walked away. He followed her.

She crossed to a bench before a nearby wine merchant's stall and sat, apparently waiting for someone. The former ship's boy then approached her. Looking elsewhere about the crowd, she didn't notice his determined advance.

"Are you Isis?" he boldly asked her.

She turned to him, surprised at being addressed by a stranger. Yet her surprise vanished when she glanced into his outstretched hand. He held forth the amulet.

"Yes," she answered him, taking the small stone piece attached to a rawhide cord. "You must be the new student. My patron said that you would meet me here."

The clever boy, not believing this, only raised his eyebrow. This response caused her to laugh. She placed the amulet about her neck, and continued.

"He often sends someone in this fashion," she explained. "I need much help, you see. We are working on a new kind of magic, and it's a most difficult task."

"But your master," he responded, not understanding, "said the counting signs were easy to learn. Once you knew their hidden meaning, of course. Is this not so?"

"True," she answered, "they are. But currently we are working on different signs. Now we devise signs for speech."

"Speech?" he repeated, taken aback. "Why? Everyone speaks."

"My patron will explain the need," she advised. "We are to meet him here, are we not? That's what usually happens."

"Yes, true enough," he concurred. "He said that we should wait for him. A short stay only."

She patted the empty space beside her on the bench. Before sitting, the boy flashed a couple of fingers to the merchant behind them. He offered a pair of cups.

"Tell me of the signs," the boy said, handing her some wine.

Before she did, the young woman first leaned over and plucked a stick from the ground.

"Why did you hold up two fingers just now?" she asked him.

"I wished a cup for both of us," he said, thinking it obvious.

"So," she mused, "this action is a symbol for the number two?"

"Yes," he agreed.

She then used her stick to scrawl three simple designs in the dirt at their sandaled feet.

"So it is with the signs," she explained to him. "These marks are symbols only. They represent the different numbers."

She pointed to the first image she'd drawn, a straight line with another shorter line attached to the left at the top. Then she moved her stick to the second, two parallel lines connected by a diagonal line. Finally, she pointed to the third, which looked much like two half diamond shapes joined one atop the other.

"Do you see?" she inquired. "These signs demonstrate exactly what they represent. The hidden secret is what they divine, for they show the numbers of angles."

"Angles?" he asked, not following.

Again she indicated the first figure she'd drawn, now making a dot where the two lines met.

"One," she instructed. "Only one angle is shown here. So, this is the sign for that number."

He nodded, now seeing the correlation.

Then she pointed to the next sign she'd drawn, which looked like what would become known as a Z shape, again making a dot where the three lines met.

"One, two," she demonstrated this time. "Just two angles are present. Therefore, this is the sign for two."

Next she poked some dots on the remaining image, again where the lines made a connection.

"One, two, three," she pointed out.

It was an easy thing to see. He was amazed. She was pleased.

"Speech will be more difficult," she observed, taking a sip of her wine. "We must make signs for different sounds. It's not as easy."

"But why?" he asked her again. "Everyone speaks, animals too. Even the lowly snake talks when hissing his warning."

"Yes," she concurred. "Snakes make a sound, sssss. Human speech has many sounds, all different, all needing a symbol."

The boy considered this rationale. He saw that it was so. Then he took her stick, and after erasing her marks with his foot, he drew a sign of his own in the dirt.

It was simple, resembling a lightning bolt striking the ground.

"This is a snake," he announced to her. "The snake makes the sssss sound, as you said. So, this is the sign for such a sound."

She looked to him, wondering where he was going. Still, she followed easily enough. She nodded her understanding.

He then drew another lightning bolt next to the first one.

"This would be two sounds," he continued, "sssss, sssss."

Again she nodded.

Next he drew a crude circle before the snakes, and then placed a small dot directly in its center.

"What is this sign?" he asked.

She didn't know. Still, the young woman was intrigued. Signs, after all, were her business.

"The sun?" she ventured.

He laughed aloud at this answer, saying, "The sun has a dot? No. This is the symbol for an eyeball which has such a distinction, as everyone easily knows."

She stared at the three signs drawn at her feet. Now she was very interested. Yet she failed to comprehend.

"This is the sign for your name," he told her, pointing with the stick at each mark in succession. "Eye, sssss, sssss. Isis."

This elegant demonstration quite astounded the young woman, and her mouth fell open. She was dumbstruck, rendered speechless. She did, however, successfully make the connection.

It could work, she realized.

"Very good," said a nearby voice.

The sitting pair looked up. The strange man who knew everything now stood beside them. The time traveler was much pleased, an easy thing to see.

"Now there will be a record," their smiling patron stated, "a rendering of what's come before. It will be fixed and unchanging. This will alter everything."

And it did.

10
The Adroit Advantage Taker
Or
The History of Turning Things Around

There once was a little man whose nearest neighbor was very clever. This neighbor had learned to split trees along the grain, a neat trick considering there were no metal tools. He used wooden wedges pounded by wooden mallets.

If that weren't enough, he'd learned to join the planks he split. He somehow notched the ends to interlock, as the fingers of your hands could. At last, employing judicious use of rawhide strips, he then invented the storage box.

This opened up lots of possibilities. Thin boxes with a strap made a strong shoulder-held carrying case while thicker boxes could be dragged, again using straps. Dogs could pull a good load this way, or people if one didn't have a dog.

But the clever man's neighbor owned a nice ox, and it was always in high demand to pull the plow of his fellow farmers. He was lucky he'd inherited it from his mother's brother, someone he'd never met. This uncle was from a distant land whose people had first tamed the massive, but now docile beasts of burden.

Years before, his mother as just a child had been taken in war, but that conflict had long ago been resolved and the unknown uncle had held no other heirs.

The hereditary ox was a marvel for, although their use was known, they were scarce and therefore hard to come by. The little man's animal was the first, and so far, the only one in the area. This rendered it a most valuable commodity.

The man's clever neighbor had made for him a big box for his ox to pull, and the large bovine could drag much with it, also a service of high demand. Yet at some point, the bottom planks of the box would always break apart under the strain. His neighbor had given him many replacements, but they broke, also.

Next he'd tried strapping hides to the bottom of the box, but while helping some, this action had failed to alleviate the problem.

This current state of affairs would soon change though, and all because of him. After much consideration, the little man now thought he knew how to remedy the situation, and it would be easy. Yes, he was very clever too, or so he thought.

Always a heavy thinker, the diminutive man, who was leading his ox that was pulling the box, came to a brook. It was hot out. He stopped to water himself and his beast, and they drank deeply.

"Are you hungry, my friend?" asked a nearby voice.

Both the ox and his startled owner looked to a tall stranger, who sat holding a large apple on the opposite bank of the gentle stream. Then the oddly dressed man held up a sack made of stitched animal skins. It was lumpy and heavy looking.

"I've aplenty," he said with a smile. "They're very sweet. Your ox would think so, too."

At this time, tasty apples were hard to come by, for not all such trees created palatable fruit. Yet, planting the seeds of those that did never produced an identical crop, instead just growing many variants. And, the knowledge of grafting vegetation, the only way to assure a standardized yield, would remain hidden for eons.

So, a while later the men sat side by side with their feet in the cool water, each one savoring an apple. The ox had already eaten three in rapid succession. Now it was more than content to stand in the brook and slowly chew his juicy cud.

The little man was explaining his big idea to the stranger and, indeed it was a simple one. Why not attach limbs to the bottom of the box? These limbs, he pointed out, would run the length of the structure, and thus keep it off the ground.

This, he was confident, would be a great improvement changing everything. The limbs would then drag the ground, not the ground on the box. What could be easier?

Yet the stranger acted as if he didn't understand, making a face and shaking his head. Of course, he did understand. He understood many things, and most were concepts the little man beside him would never know, or even know of.

This stranger was a stranger in more ways than one for, unknown to his companion, he was in fact a time traveler currently occupied with a critical mission.

He picked up a flat rock and handed it to the little man. Then reaching about, he picked up two short, nearly straight sticks. These he handed over, also.

"Show me," he requested.

The little man placed the sticks parallel on the ground between them. Then he put the rock atop them. Next he demonstrated, by sliding the rock over the twigs.

"Problem eliminated," he pronounced, pleased with himself.

"This is good," the stranger agreed. But then, after taking a bite of his apple, he added, "I see another way, though. It's a much better way of pulling things."

"How? he was asked.

The determined time traveler took hold of the rock. Instead of sliding it over the sticks as his companion had done, he moved it the other way. He pushed it against the twigs, which now both twirled neatly underneath it.

"You'd use logs," he advised. "You and your helper just need to find some way to attach them. Is this not a better solution?"

Making the connection, the little man agreed, and said so.

He soon hurried off most anxious to try out this novel idea, naturally to be claimed as his own innovation. His clever friend, he knew, would somehow work out any complicated details. So, he pulled on his ox that pulled the box.

The contented stranger, still eating his apple, watched them go.

11
The Woman Who Changed Everything
Or
A Brief History of Beans

Even as a child, things that grew had fascinated her. Of course, as gathering wild plants was within the female realm, this was fortunate. Other women in the tribe were good at the task, as she became, but she really enjoyed it, as well.

When the foraging parties had left each morning, she dashed ahead, eager, anticipating. If the gathering was good, the women's baskets were soon full and the young girl was then free to roam on her own. She used that time to look at plants.

It didn't matter if they weren't edible. Often the most captivating ones she found were not. She just liked things that grew, for they were always interesting.

As a toddler too young to gather, her chores had included helping, as best she could, the older women as they engaged in cleaning in and about the family's tent. This involved tagging along as the toothless ones dumped the garbage at one of the various pits the tribe used for the purpose. It was there that the young girl had first noticed the newborn growing things, struggling to live at the pit's edge.

Why would plants live in such a smelly place, she wondered? Still, they did, pushing their spindly stalks to the sun. They even moved their new, tender leaves towards its direction, and how did the growing things know to do this?

133

Later, after turning old enough to forage, she discerned even more intriguing things, details the others didn't notice or care about. They couldn't be bothered for their only concern was filling their baskets, and looking at things that you couldn't eat held no fascination for them. She, however, was always captivated.

Her primitive tribe of hunter-gathers had no permanent home but perpetually moved about, yet often as not, if the local game was plentiful and the men and their dogs successful in the hunt, it stayed put for more than a season at a time. And, when this did happen, through all the year the inquisitive girl had carefully noted each change occurring in the growing things. Soon, no matter the season, she could predict what would happen to them next, and she was always proved correct.

A few times, while still very young, she tried to grow plants but this had never been successful. She'd dug holes and placed sprouts from the pit's edge into them, but the plants had perished, drying up in days. Then she'd tried planting them closer to the river but these, having little sun, also died.

Undaunted, on the next occasion she once more planted in the sun, but this time she watered the sprouts.

A neighbor boy she knew, whose father was headman of her clan, thought this whole idea very foolish. Why work to grow something that grew elsewhere? What was the purpose, given you could just go out and find it?

Still, she persisted and carried out her idea. Because the boy liked her, he feigned interest, and he even helped her tote the water. But the experiment proved inconclusive, for the tribe had traveled on before the outcome became apparent.

She resolved to try again once the proper conditions permitted, but thinking in this next effort of using a different kind of plant.

In the meantime, her life moved forward, as did her wandering tribe. Once the boy became a man, he took her, now a fine woman, as his mate. They were happy.

She quickly became a mother several times over, and for a while this halted her excursions. Yet she never forgot her plan. In fact, she thought of it often as her offspring aged, for each reminded her of how the plants also grew and changed.

When her children were toddlers she resumed her foraging, for they could now accompany her. However, as they demanded much attention, she had no free time to implement her long simmering idea. Yet, once adolescents they began to have chores about the camp, and this at last allowed her to consider it again.

The tribe's currently claimed area turned out to be bountiful, and the tribal elders, who were the headmen from each clan, announced their decision to stay for as many seasons as the abundant game continued to thrive. So, the young woman judged the time to try once more might never be better. But what growing thing, she constantly wondered, would she endeavor to cultivate in this newest attempt?

Then, one day late in the afternoon, she discovered a peaceful meadow cut by a lazy stream encircled and hidden by the deep, surrounding forest. The open field was thickly covered with many vines that twisted and climbed amidst each other. From long experience she easily recognized these plants, now in full flower.

Soon, she knew, these vines would bear pods, and these pods would then grow the tasty beans so prized by her kind. She also knew that other gatherers would take them if they could, even before they were ripe, for everyone in the tribe enjoyed their hearty flavor. Therefore, the young woman told no one of her find.

Every few days she went back to assess the bean plants, knowing that once the pods ripened they would soon pop open.

When they did, of course, the beans were released and fell to the ground, thus becoming harder to gather. So, each day she tried to pick the ripest pods just before they popped, correctly judging from both familiarity and long experience the most opportune moment to harvest them.

Indeed, they were very tasty.

As the pods ripened at various times, her harvest continued for several weeks, but soon almost all of them were gone. She noticed, however, a few of the plants had pods that although ripe had failed to open, as if to protect the beans inside. Finally, when the days turned cold, she picked these now hardened pods, as well.

Yet, she didn't cook the now sleeping beans they held.

She put these pods, only a handful, in a hollowed-out gourd she used for storage. From time to time she'd crack one open, finding the beans in perfect condition. Once the weather warmed, her long considered plan was fully formed.

She picked a sunny hillside not far from her tent, and set her children to clearing an area sufficient to accommodate her beans, now seeds of the next generation, which numbered well over twice the amount of all her fingers. She then scattered them about, lightly covering them against the birds that also appreciated their delicious flavor. She carefully watered them, and waited.

Yet they did not grow. She resolved to find out why. She then dug up a few and examined them.

They still seemed perfect, and she was confused. Next she decided to visit the original meadow, to see if any beans were growing there this season. None were, but she found something else in the clearing, something quite unexpected.

A strange man, not of her tribe, was there. She abruptly stopped, leery once she finally saw him sitting in the meadow. Yet he only smiled sweetly, and nodded.

She thought of running away, but she didn't. She sensed no danger, oddly none at all and, after a bit she stepped closer, now only wondering who he was. At her steady, determined approach, the strange man slowly stood.

He was thin and very tall. He was also dressed strangely, and wore garments unlike any that she had ever seen. No clan she knew of had such a covering.

"Welcome," he said to her, "I've been waiting for you."

This statement she didn't believe. Still, she laughed a bit, for he was a man and she thought him only flirting, as most men would do with any unattended female. Yet the stranger politely persisted, quickly dispelling her misplaced conclusion.

"The ground remains cold," he informed her, "too cold for your still sleeping seeds. Just have patience. It won't be long."

Following this profound pronouncement, she did become wary. The feeling, however, was fleeting and soon passed. She looked him in the face, now highly curious.

"How do you know such?" she asked of him.

The man bid her to sit. He sat also, across from her. Then he smiled again, in reassurance.

"I know many things," he answered her. "I know of your long interest, and of your newest intent. And," he added for emphasis, "I also know your vision is a true one."

At this, she smiled at him, for under the bizarre circumstances she was compelled to accept this stranger at his word. It was an easy thing for her to do. The woman still didn't know who he was or why he was helping her, but nevertheless she somehow understood that he had only her best interests in mind.

Indeed he did. He was most eager to assist her, it was his singular goal. The tall stranger was from another Timeframe, and aiding her was his direct mission.

Soon the beans grew. Every evening, she checked on them after her daily chores had been seen to, and shortly others in her clan took notice, as well. Her mate was much amused by all this attention, seeing no real value in her self-imposed, added labors.

Nevertheless, the beans thrived in a perfect growing season. Nothing went amiss. The rain was always gentle and no pest, insect nor animal, attacked her plants.

Now more than her clan was engrossed. Word was spreading. The local men who came to gawk were well entertained by all the heavy interest, as her mate had been, but the hard-working women in the tribe saw and appreciated the inherent advantages.

They offered their help.

The young woman politely refused. Their labor was currently unneeded, she knew. The strange man in the meadow had explained everything in detail.

"Maybe next year," she said.

Her bean plants soon produced a bumper crop. When this happened, word really spread. Even the most hardened of the tribal men were impressed, for they all loved beans as much as meat, and now they saw the obvious advantage, too.

Beans, after all, while being quite an enjoyable meal were generally hard to come by.

The young woman shared her bounty with her clan, and her mate shared in the gratitude that followed. He was most proud of her. Undeniably, she was a good woman.

She did ask her female kinfolk for help in shelling the beans. It was a big task taking much time, for there were many full baskets of pods. The women sat in a circle as they worked and talked of the future, laughing together at every opportunity.

The beans were carefully graded before being doled out. Many of them were an average size or smaller, and these were the ones equally divided and dispersed, a most succulent bonus. A substantial number, however, were bigger than the average, and the woman kept these back to plant in the next season.

The next season never came. The tribe, after two years, moved on. Sadly, its new territory was heavily wooded and held no area sufficiently suitable for her beans.

She and her mate then argued over them. He wanted to eat her tasty seeds, and he boldly stated they would go bad if they didn't. She'd always check first, but after finding them still only sleeping, each time she stiffly refused to comply.

Then, in the warming time the tribe suddenly returned to its previous location. The cautious elders now judged moving a hasty mistake. The available game was still plentiful and there was abundant water to be had close by.

The woman staked her rawhide tent by her old, sunny hillside.

Now they came, scores of women from many clans in the tribe. Their mates all wanted tasty beans. Teach us, they pleaded, the secrets of how to grow them.

She did, but she demanded a price. The women would learn by tending her plot, under her instructions, some of every day for a season. She would initiate them, and also give them beans to plant, but only after her harvest was completed.

This was a stiff bargain. Men didn't like waiting. More importantly, they wouldn't understand such a strange arrangement, and they'd only see their women working for someone else, an unheard of thing.

The now fully mature and resolute woman replied only, "If we start soon, and the early air is warm enough, we can have two harvests. Your men will have beans later, in the cooling times, but still this season. Or," she casually added, "only my clan will assist me now, and next season you can ask them for help."

The tribe's women saw wisdom in this, for it was a good plan. Enlightening their mates would be a different matter. Still, after using her argument, they did.

This time, there were problems. First there was too much rain, and later the fat, green bugs arrived. Luckily, many men, always impatient for beans, came by to check on things and ended up eating most of the juicy insects.

Some plants did die, but many more survived and again there was a bumper crop. As earlier stipulated, the growing season was only halfway done and the mentoring woman then held to her part of the bargain, dispersing seed to her now trained, former helpers. All were excited, and they eagerly rushed home to quickly create their own, small garden plots.

After her second course of beans was planted, she returned to the hidden meadow in hopes that the strange man would still be there. He was. Again they sat.

"You've done much good," he told her, "I knew that you would."

"Yes," the woman concurred, "this is a fine thing for the tribe, but I'm most concerned. There are times that I cannot grow tasty beans, for often the forest is too thick and the sun is blocked. Tell me how to raise my plants then."

The time traveler answered quietly, saying, "You must grow your beans in a new and different way. You must have fine fields, always. Your tribe should not move but always stay, and grow many beans in many fine fields."

"But men hunt," she answered him. "They follow the prey to do so. The tribe will move, it will always move, it must."

"You can trade for meat," was his rejoinder, "for other tribes will savor your tasty beans, too. Many tribes would gladly trade good meat for good beans. And your men will be busy with another thing, a vital thing they must do now."

"What thing," she asked, "helping grow beans?"

"Not yet," he instructed. "That will come later, but for now the men must do something else of great importance. They must protect the ones that grow the beans."

This she understood. Why work for something when it can be taken by force? Many unfriendly tribes would want beans and, not yet knowing how to grow them, they would try to steal them instead, why wouldn't they?

Still, she had reservations.

"The tribe will always stay," she asked him, "for beans alone? No, this is too great of a change. This would change everything."

The stranger slowly nodded, understanding her dilemma. Yet, he also knew that it was just a matter of time. Change always comes, and time will out, regardless.

"Your beans first came from wild beans here," he said, with a sweep of his arm, indicating the meadow now full of fine grass.

"Yes," she agreed.

"Yet, if you didn't take them," he continued, "the pods would have just popped open, with the beans falling to the ground."

"Yes," she said again.

"The beans do this to live," he said, "so that other beans will come later. But some pods didn't pop open. Their beans, being trapped, could not grow."

"Yes," she said for a third time.

"But now they do grow," he pointed out. "They can live because of you. These beans will now feed your tribe, and other plants do much the same thing."

Again he indicated the field around them. The tall grass was full of tiny, green seed heads. Strange, she hadn't noticed them before and she should have.

This particular type of grass was a most delicious plant, too.

"This seed must be taken early, before it's ripe," he explained. "If not, it will just fall from the stalk in order to grow the next grass. It's hard to gather then."

Here she only nodded, knowing from experience it was true.

"But, like your beans," he said, "some stalks will keep their tasty seeds. They won't fall like the others do. These seeds would never grow, for once the stalk finally fell, the ground itself would then be too cold to welcome them."

"I see it," she said, but then she made the larger connection.

The man, realizing this by the look on her face, smiled.

"This grass can also be grown?" she inquired.

"Easily," he answered, "but plant only the ones with the largest seeds, like you did with your beans. Some of the new seed will be larger still, and you will then save this to plant. Much food can thus be grown and traded by your tribe."

She traveled home, enthused, but still her mind was troubled. How could she, only a woman, convince the stiff elders to always stay and grow things? She knew not.

Yet, once at her tent she found that great change had already arrived. The clan's headman, her mate's father, had died suddenly in the night. The clan members had quickly elected the dead man's son, her mate, to replace him.

Now her mate was the headman of her clan, and so by extension a member of the tribe's elders as well, albeit the youngest and most inexperienced.

"We must always stay," she told him. She then explained the reasons why, the same rationalities the strange man had listed. But her mate was noncommittal.

Trying to sway him, she returned many times to the meadow to pick the ripest seed heads there, for he loved the sweet loafs they always made. The smell of them cooking alone was mesmerizing. Still, he didn't agree to always stay.

Each time the determined woman returned to gather, she wished again to speak to the stranger, but she never did. She couldn't. He wasn't there.

One day when the cooling times came, she stood surveying her bean field. The dying plants were now bare of pods, for they had all been harvested. Because of her unwavering efforts, the plot was now just one of many in the tribe and this season they had all produced many tasty beans.

Her mate, returning from the day's hunt, then approached her.

"When will you tell the elders to always stay?" she demanded.

He sighed, not wanting to argue further.

"To always stay may be a good idea," he conceded, "but it's a new idea. And I'm a new elder. They would not listen to me."

"You are my man," she said slowly, her eyes hard and her jaw set, "and you should see this my way, it makes good sense. Beans keep, meat does not. They will feed us when the cold comes, a good thing if the hunting is bad."

This statement shocked him at first for he took it as an affront, a commentary on his competence as a provider, but that reaction soon passed. She was a good woman. She spoke the truth and undeniably it was a noble point.

What's more, he hadn't even considered this view, a valid advantage. That rankled for as an elder, even a novice one, he always needed to contemplate every option. Yet now, the hard-pressed man only grunted, turned and walked away.

She turned also, back to her dead beans. What else could she do? She didn't know.

Much later he returned to the tent, holding a solemn face.

"I talked to the elders," he announced. "They agree to always stay, at least for now. The tribe can still move later, if need be."

Her eyes filled with tears and he took her in his arms. Then she cried outright. Next, her mate tightly hugged her.

"Good thing," he whispered, "they all love beans."

Before the cold time started in earnest, she returned to the meadow. The strange man was not there. Something else was though, a gift from him, perhaps.

She noticed dark brown, fully ripened seed heads on several of the grass stalks. These seeds had not been broadcast. She gathered them and then walked home.

To always stay.

12
How it all Started
Or
The Short History of Dogs

The young upright man, in reality still only a boy, had smelled the cooking meat from quite a distance. It was compelling. The wafting aroma was mesmerizing, faint at first but unmistakable, growing only stronger with each tentative step that he took, tearing away at his empty stomach, forcing him ever forward.

Finding himself in unfamiliar territory, the youngster was understandably leery, but also being very hungry he continued through the thick underbrush with a determined purpose, in an unending quest. He knew he had to find nourishment or he would die. Then who would tell his strange story?

He'd eaten little the day before, too agitated by the gathering to come, for it was the first such endeavor that he'd ever been permitted to accompany. Due to his tender age, before this his never-ending chores of toting water from the river, or dragging tree limbs for the ever-present fire had always been in close proximity to his clan's current, well-defendable enclosure. No excitement there, to be sure.

Of course, the youth had often longed to join in one these gatherings, seemingly a hopeless wish, given his tender years. Still, he dreamed of the day for it was his undeniable path, as it was for each of the clan's boys. His time would come.

Then, on one of his last wood collecting expeditions he'd found a heavy branch that made for him, with little augmentation, a fine club. All of the mature upright men had admired this new weapon, hefting and swinging it, testing its strength and balance. Each had been impressed by the unexpected discovery.

His uncle, headman of the clan, was most pleased, taking the find as an omen predicting a plentiful gathering. As a consequence, he allowed his nephew to join the upcoming venture. Sadly, this snap assessment had proved a mistake.

All gatherings were, and always had been unpredictable things, the outcomes ever in doubt. Still, the clan's most recent location was extremely bountiful and of late all such expeditions had indeed been successful. Each time the upright men had returned from them both cheerful and fully laden with meat.

The gathering party took to the great river before dawn, paralleling its meandering path, following the clan's standard operating procedure. Several times along the way the uprights noticed promising footprints of the four legs at the water's edge, an event that engendered much interest. However, nothing came of them as they petered out once the ground became firmer inland from the river's bank, and so the determined party had returned each time to its previous route.

Gathering from the four legs was the best possible scenario for they could be beaten off their kill with little trouble. Often this kill was a large animal. The four legs were formidable, always hunting in numbers that employed coordinated attack, and this strategy was highly effective in bringing almost anything down.

Yet, if they were attacked with sufficient preparation, successfully employing the tactics of surprise and overwhelming forces, the four legs would quickly relent and run off. The gathering party would then divide their efforts. Some would butcher while the others stood guard, encircling the kill, protecting the periphery of the grisly action.

The four legs always took a dim view of this, of course. They never retreated very far at first, but hung at a distance growling and snapping at each other in their displeasure over losing their kill. At some point though, compelled by hunger, they would be off in search of more game, and often this occurred before the meaty prize had been hacked into smaller pieces suitable for transport.

Other hunters in the area, such as the deadly long claws, were not so obliging. They were to be avoided at all times, for backing down and running away wasn't in their fierce nature. No, they attacked to protect their kill, and they were much larger, highly aggressive and so more dangerous than the four legs were.

Fortunately, their deeply resonate growl and loud, piercing cries could be heard at great distance and usually the ferocious creatures could be given a wide berth. Of course, this was not always possible and chance meetings sometimes occurred. When they did, the standard outcome never favored the upright men.

The long claws had very long teeth, too.

The clan's ancestors had learned all these hard-earned lessons well, ages ago in the olden times. They hadn't been forgotten in the great interim since. Many well-known and oft repeated stories told of such horrifying encounters.

No, the four legs were clearly the best choice and the clan always preferred gathering from them, but where were they now?

Late in the day and far from home, the weary upright men turned a sharp bend in the river only to find there a large horned one lying dead on the bank. Nothing seemed to be near it, although it was evident that the fresh carcass had been fed upon. The group advanced with alacrity to investigate, but only when they were up on the beast did the shocking truth become known.

Behind it, shielded by its very size, rested two sleeping cubs of the terrifying great one of the forest. This was a most surprising turn having frightening consequences, for before the upright men could react, the cubs' mother broke from the nearby scrub. Very large and bristling, she was already snarling in anger at this intrusion, berserk now in her attempt to protect her young ones.

The startled party was no match for her massive claws and great bulk. Several of them were immediately mauled before they could move away, and more were quickly run down and dispatched as her cubs, awakened by the unknown sounds, began crying loudly in fear. This event propelled their mother into a true frenzy, and she viciously lashed out unhindered by any thought, fueled only by her terrible rage.

The young upright boy, proudly clutching his fine new club, had been among the first gatherers to reach the dead horned one. Soon he was caught with a tremendous, backhanded blow from the giant, swinging paw of the great one of the forest, who was madly thrashing about consumed by her impassioned slaughtering. It was as if a tree had hit him, and he was thrown unceremoniously into the great river.

This alone had saved him.

Of course, the youth couldn't swim, none of the upright men could. The always churning and never-ending river was very much viewed as a mystical thing by the clan, and so they had yet to even learn how to fish. But the boy, stunned, had nevertheless somehow floated to a passing log that bore him downstream, and thus away from the horrid carnage still viciously transpiring on the now overly-bloodied and gory bank.

After some time of desperately clutching about the log, he was rudely deposited ashore after his transport was beached while traversing a long bend in the river. The exhausted youngster had pulled himself further up on the bank and collapsed in a heap. It was then that he smelled the cooking meat in the distance.

Naturally he was unsure of his location, but that didn't matter. He had to eat soon or he would never live to find his way home, if that were even possible now. He began to move, honing in on the enticing scent of roasting flesh.

Evening was near, and approaching swiftly. Soon he wouldn't be able to discern anything in the quickly growing gloom. Next, however, he saw the piercing light of a fire in the distance, shrouded by the surrounding forest.

The calling aroma was strong now. It turned his empty stomach into knots. He crept closer taking care to move as quietly as he could, always forward towards the illumination beyond, which at this point was enveloped by the deepening darkness.

At last he could see the entire scene through the underbrush. A fine campsite had been laid in a small clearing rimmed by huge boulders. A giant fire, blazing away, cast flickering shadows against the rocks and shrubbery around them.

He saw no one about. It seemed the whole area was deserted. He did see the meat though, sizzling on a spit very near the fire, a huge hunk dripping tasty fat.

Who would leave such a treasure unattended?

Instinctively he reached for his sharpened butchering stone, a most valued object that everyone carried during a gathering, a highly-prized implement carefully chiseled with precision to fit the owner's hand. He found it missing as was, of course, his fine new club. He should have realized that the unforgiving waterway had already swallowed both of his precious tools.

The young upright man next judged himself not only lost and alone, which he was, but now totally weaponless as well.

Yet here he was wrong.

His finest instrument, possessed by every member of his clan as well as those scattered about like them, had been minutely honed through time itself, from the very beginnings of his kind. It was a natural development unique to the now fully defined species, and no other living thing possessed it. Nothing came close, not even the lumbering, flat-headed men in the area who were generally so similar to the uprights.

This singular, superior weapon, at present being furiously employed to assess the situation, was his very large human brain.

This particular circumstance, however, was difficult to understand. Where was the owner of the meat, he wondered? And why had they left such an item unprotected?

Upright men cooked their food, of course, but they weren't the only ones to do so. The flatheads had fire as well, and they, according to the clan's ancient lore, were the ones who'd first unlocked its hidden secrets. And they could be fearsome.

At last he could stand it no longer. He broke through the brush and dashed to the spit, thinking only at first of grabbing the roasting meat and beating a hasty retreat. Yet, after laying hands on the greasy haunch, he instead had a much better idea.

The boy sank to his knees and bit into the still sizzling flesh. Nothing had ever tasted so good to him, and he moaned in delight as the succulent juices dripped down his face. Despite his earlier trepidation, he sat by the fire and ate with gusto, unconcerned now with what might happen next.

After savoring several mouthfuls he reconsidered, thinking again of dashing off with his purloined meal, but he didn't. He was so exhausted he found that he couldn't move, only concentrate on the task at hand. He reasoned if the food's owner did return and killed him, well at least by then he'd die with a full stomach.

While munching away, he heard movement in the brush, the sound of someone approaching. The youngster, still chewing as fast as he could, sat in place and awaited his fate. At this stage, no other viable option was left open to him.

An upright man then appeared, but unlike any that he'd ever seen before. He was very tall, as tall as a flathead, but unlike them he was thin and dressed in a bizarre fashion. He wore no stitched animal skins but some kind of covering that aside from his hands and face totally wrapped him, clinging tightly to his body.

"Welcome," he said, but the boy didn't respond.

The newcomer then held out his arms, his palms open and pointed toward the youngster, who had stopped his mastication at the action. After a few seconds, the strange upright man dropped his hands. Then he smiled.

"Welcome," he said again, and this time the interloper replied.

"I'm hungry," the young boy related, as if that would explain everything. It did. The upright man smiled again, and then sat on a large stone at the edge of the firelight.

"I know," he answered. "I cooked it for you. I knew that you'd make your way here, to this clearing, tonight."

The boy's eyes opened widely as he considered this. Could it be so? Then with a shrug he commenced his meal, knowing now that no immediate danger awaited him.

Yet, after swallowing his latest mouthful, he asked, "How?"

Now the sitting man considered. He rearranged himself and, crossing his long legs, he leaned forward. After a bit he answered.

"I know much," he stated as a fact. "I know that today was your first gathering, and I know the result. This adventure will make for you a fine story to tell."

At this the boy only grunted. How would he ever get back to his clan, and how would he tell his story if he didn't? He knew not.

Again he sunk his teeth into the roast but without frenzy now, in a slower and more deliberate pace, still thinking.

The stranger spoke no more, for the present only waiting for the boy to finish his meal. The man understood that the youngster's mind was racing, trying to comprehend. He was content to sit and let him try.

Soon enough the upright boy was satiated, his stomach now overly full. Still chewing his last bite, he stared down at the meat in his hands. Then he held it out to the stranger, offering the leftovers but the man shook his head, declining.

"Take it with you, on the morrow," he said. "Just head back to the river and follow its bank, moving against the current this time. You'll be home by nightfall."

The boy nodded. It made sense. He would do so.

Then he thought of something else.

"What of the others?" he asked. Of course, this question referred to the ambushed gathering party. Here the man, while giving no answer, answered all by his silence.

The boy sighed, already knowing the truth. He'd reflected on the horrific episode while clinging to the log in the river. The great one of the forest was the most fearsome thing known, and the females were ever tenacious when their cubs were involved.

He thought first of his uncle, and then the others, the best uprights in his clan, each gone. Who would gather now? How would they ever survive this loss?

The strange man knew his thoughts. He felt sorry for the boy, but only in a peripheral, disconnected fashion. He had to remain above the fray, so to speak.

After all, time does march on, and always it will have its due.

"Other clans would welcome you," he said, in a comforting tone. "Your women and children are a wonderful asset, and greater numbers help insure the future. You must lead them, your clan, to another clan, and so save them."

The young upright was rendered speechless by this bold suggestion. How could he lead them, or what was left of them? He was just a boy, lost and helpless.

"You now have a powerful story," instructed the man, "for there's a grander purpose behind it. It has meaning beyond the event itself, a lesson to be learned. So they will listen and agree with your assessment, why wouldn't they?"

"What purpose?" asked the incredulous youth, who certainly saw none. The whole thing was senseless as far as he could judge, the gathering nothing but a colossal failure. He boldly looked the man in the face, awaiting an answer.

"You must change the way you gather meat," said the stranger, as if it were only a foregone conclusion. "Another way must be found. A better way."

A moment went by, the boy deep in thought.

"How?" he asked for a second time.

The strange man then slowly stood and, after holding out his hands in reassurance, he stepped over and sat closer to the boy.

"Why do you always chase the four legs away?" he quietly asked. "They are the ones that find your meat, after all. Do you not have to go out and waste your time locating them all over again, come the next gathering?"

Now the youngster was really confused. How could you not chase them away? The hard-earned carcass was their prize and they didn't give it up freely.

He began to answer as such, but the man cut him off by continuing, "Why not instead give them some of the kill? It's easily done for they never run far, and you know this to be true. You could just throw them some of the meat."

"Why?" blurted the boy. "It's our food then. Why give it away?"

Again, the stranger smiled, understanding the boy's perplexed state. Change once made could take hold quickly, but embracing this choice often required great time to accomplish. Yet, small steps were still forward progress.

"But if you gave them some they would stick close by," he explained, "and they'd gladly follow you home if you fed them along the way. Then you wouldn't have to find them when the meat was gone. Once you stop feeding them they'd just go off in search of more, yet you could then follow them, is this not so?"

"But they are killers," said the boy, now the one trying to explain. How, he marveled, could such an absurd thing even be contemplated? This was not the established way.

"But do they kill," asked the man, "after they're chased off? Do they attack you as you butcher the carcass, as the long claws would? No, they just get angry and then move on."

156

The boy shook his head. This was too much. It was unheard of.

"That's never done," he stated flatly, as if it closed the subject.

Again, the stranger paused. Another approach was needed now, that much was evident. He held one in reserve, of course.

He leaned in some and quietly asked, "How did the upright men first come by fire, I wonder? There was a distant age, long ago, when you had none, is this not true? Many stories from the olden times say as much, do they not?"

The boy had to admit that this was so. Everyone knew that the uprights had stolen fire from the flatheads, for they were the only ones who knew how to make it. As such, keeping the fire lit was always a prime concern for the clan.

Sometimes it did go out, of course, a big problem. Other clans had to share then, but they only did so after some price had been paid. Finding fire in the forest was always possible, it had happened before, but it wasn't very likely and the more prudent course was to make sure that it never died in the first place.

But the boy, young as he was, had made this vital connection. Things change. Even the oldest of established ways must have been new once, he currently saw.

Yes, now he understood that change was very real, and perhaps inevitable. The day's bizarre events had proved as much. And he certainly didn't wish to repeat that particular change if he could help it, not if it could be avoided, that is.

So, he mused after reflection, "Perhaps this would be better."

Then the young boy causally made another, most crucial connection. It was one that went beyond the moment at hand, critical as it turned out, to the very future of his entire species. This simple thought pattern had profound historic ramifications, for the conception easily defined by example the most important, pertinent tenant of humanity itself.

"Well," he said at last, "I guess I'll never know unless I try."

It turned out that he did try, and he succeeded, too. Once his decimated clan had effectively joined with another, the novel procedure was instigated and it proved most advantageous. The four legs indeed followed the gathering uprights home, and they hung close by until the meat was gone, as predicted.

Gatherings then became hugely profitable. After the clan took to the forest, almost at once the four legs would find a scent and, with little trouble they would then run some prey aground. Meat was thus found every day.

There were also other benefits to the new arrangement.

The four legs were wonderful sentries. Nothing in the night could creep up on them or, by extension, the clan. They still kept their distance, but the animals inherently understood the advantages too, and they protected them.

Living near the upright men supplied a safe environment in which to raise their young. True, their kill was taken from them, but the meat they were always given was enough, and this was their main concern. They stayed.

There were only five of them at first, a small pack consisting of an alpha couple and three juveniles, two males and one female. Soon enough more pups followed. This was viewed as a good omen by the clan, and it was.

Then, after several seasons had passed, the four legs one night raised a cry in the dark. The hair-raising shrieks of the long claws were soon heard in the distance. A loud altercation then ensued, very brief but brutal, then all was quiet.

The next morning the boy, who was now a strapping teenager, found at some distance a dead four legs, lacerated by the long claws. Her pack was nowhere to be seen, having run off in angry pursuit in order to harass the retreating perpetrator. The boy was unconcerned by this as they often ran off and, he knew from experience that they would soon return, demanding more meat.

It was then that he discovered the pups, newly orphaned and whimpering in the grass. They were young, hardly weaned, and almost without thinking he took them inside the clan's fortified enclosure. They became instant celebrities.

Again they were five, four brothers and a sister. They snapped and growled much, but due to their tiny size they posed no real problems. That soon changed.

The two largest males, angling for dominance, became a danger because they consistently wished to demonstrate their fierceness. Within weeks the boy, again without a thought, clubbed them both. That left two males and the female.

These pups grew and in time joined the pack outside the upright's base. While not really tame, at a distance they interacted much more with the clan, and were even permitted entry into their enclosure if they wished. They were easily tolerated there, if not provoked by being approached too closely or quickly.

Once the young female bore pups, being proud, she brought them in for inspection, and they became instant celebrities, too.

Again the boy, now a man in earnest, clubbed the most vicious babies, and the offspring of the tamer survivors were more tolerant still. This now, entrenched protocol continued unabated. By the fifth generation, taking less than ten full seasons, the newest born pups, while hunting every day in the forest, stayed every night within the enclosure, content if still irascible at times.

The boy, currently a fully mature man, realized they now preferred the company of the uprights to their wilder kin, still ensconced at the encampment's edge.

Ten more seasons came and went. The boy, having lived nearly thirty years, was now an old man. He had many good dogs by then, and they all loved him.

One day he sat on the great river's broad bank. The scene was idyllic, shaded with the air neither hot nor cold, but he was thinking of another instance along the water's edge. That particular time, he recalled, had not been so pleasant.

He was remembering the day it had all started.

Then he heard someone approaching and the strange, upright man appeared, stepping from the brush. He looked exactly the same, as if the passing seasons had no hold on him. They didn't, of course, for he was a time traveler.

"Well, my friend," he said to the one who was once only a lost and hungry boy, "you have done much good work. I knew that you would. Does it please you?"

The old one, pausing to consider, reached over and scratched the ear of his nearest companion, which wagged its tail in response to the tender action. Then the upright realized that none of his dogs, before ever vigilant, had reacted in the least to the stranger's advance. Yet upon short reflection, given the context, he knew this wasn't a surprising circumstance.

"I am content," he announced at last, "for the clan has much meat. And I'm amazed that the dogs now love and protect us. So yes, I'm very pleased that a change was made, and that it was you who found me in the forest so long ago."

This sentiment caused the time traveler to laugh aloud. He sat near to the upright, as he had done the last time. Then he caressed the dog stretched prone between them.

Again the animal wagged its tail, thumping slowly this time.

"But you were the one who found me," the tall man pointed out. "You could have given up in the river, or at its bank. Yet you didn't relent, only bravely pushed on."

The old man hunched his shoulders, replying, "I was hungry."

They both enjoyed this banter, each chuckling some.

After a time the old man asked, "What will happen now?"

"More change," was the time traveler's answer. "It is always so. It will always be so, forever."

The old man nodded, knowing it was true.

"But how?" he probed, wishing clarification. "What new changes come? What will happen next?"

The stranger leaned in, again as he had done at their last encounter, and after a bit he answered with, "The upright man is a strong animal, and he thinks. Now he can hunt, not just gather. So, he can provide for, and protect himself well."

The old one nodded.

"But when an upright man takes himself a family," came next, "he will always protect them, too."

The old one nodded again, adding, "Yes."

"The families of his kin are also his family," the stranger next explained, "for they are related, and when many such families join they become a clan, as yours did. Each member of this clan is now also his kin, for they are all connected in some way. So a man will protect his clan as well as his own, for they are the same."

"Yes," the old one said once more.

"Now," the man said, "you have dogs in your family, and they will protect you too, for they are a true part of your clan, as well. Because of them, your clan will become much stronger. Other clans will do this also, and then all clans will grow stronger."

"I see it," nodded the old one, but next he saw something else. It was another correlation. He didn't like its portent, but still he understood it well enough.

"They will squabble with each other for the best meat," he predicted. "They will fight over the finer ground that has it. And soon they will club each other to acquire it, in order to provide for, and so protect their family."

"Yes," the stranger concurred, but then he added, "Yet, at some point certain clans will join together, forming a tribe, and things will be very different then."

The upright man was surprised by this assertion.

"These new tribes, they will not fight each other?" he asked.

"No, they will fight," was the answer, "that's not my meaning. I mean that tribes fight for a different reason, a new reason. Tribe members will do battle for those not related to them, for in tribes there are many that aren't connected by family ties."

This concept once more took the old one aback. Who would fight for those who weren't related? Then he thought of his beloved dogs, so different from the upright men and he understood, again making the proper connection.

Next, once seeing the consequences, the old man expanded upon them. Yes, he easily sensed the broader implications involved. His very large human brain, ancient by current standards still worked, and it worked very well.

"Such new tribes, after growing ever stronger, will then band together?" he asked of the stranger.

"In the far future, yes," was the answer. "Tribes become states, and states become mighty nations. The strongest of these nations will grow further still, becoming vast empires."

The old man was amazed by this insightful declaration. It was a great vision, no doubting that. He was humbled.

The stranger slowly stood, and added, "All because of the dogs, my friend. It will happen because you made this vital connection and took them in. Everything now changes because you tried something different by thinking in a new and unexpected way."

The astounded upright sighed after this lofty pronouncement. He turned to look at the time traveler before him. Again he hunched his shoulders, adding a wistful smile.

"I was hungry," he reiterated, as if that explained everything.

It did, and the tall stranger then walked away for the last time.

Notes on Context

Hardware employed in **Part One** of this book is detailed in the first Epic Fable of Time, **Beyond the Elastic Limit**, and various missions to correct the altered Timeline are fully covered in the second Epic Fable of Time, **Piercing the Elastic Limit**.

Historic figures mentioned in **Part Two** of this collection are genuine, and the circumstances surrounding them are accurately portrayed; for example: Archimedes of Syracuse was indeed murdered after his doomed city fell, the events of the ill-fated Battle of the Solent took place as described, William Clark did send fossils to President Jefferson as depicted, and Albert Einstein's father truly was a pioneering electrical engineer.

As stated, if after **Part Three** the Timeline was corrected, then by definition and from current perspective, any successful alterations to the flow have already taken place.

Ergo, no recorded reality of this former Timeframe exists outside these Epic Fables.

Acknowledgements

To Steph, for the third time never failing.

Many thanks to Nancy, my Star Editor.

Thanks also to Julia, Fran and once more Virginia, who patiently read each chapter as they materialized.

I'm most grateful to Bill, who discussed plot lines along the way.

And again to Rob, technically consummate as always.

44874427R00096

Made in the USA
Charleston, SC
10 August 2015